BOARDING

ELISE FABER

BOARDING
BY ELISE FABER
Newsletter sign-up

BOARDING

Copyright © 2019 Elise Faber
Print ISBN-13: 978-1-946140-19-7
Ebook ISBN-13: 978-1-946140-18-0
Cover Art by Jena Brignola

ACKNOWLEDGMENTS

Thank you so much to my fabulous editors, Julie, Kay, and Christine for helping me bring this story to life. I can't tell you how much I rely on you guys to make my stories palatable

To my family. Thanks for supporting me, for letting me bounce different sentence structures, commas, synonyms, and plot points off all of you. I couldn't write without your help and also your help in leaving me alone so I CAN write. I love you very much.

To my fan group, the Fabinators. Thanks for being so awesome and loving my books and just generally brightening my day. Jaci and Johanna, thanks for keeping the group lively and engaging.

And to you, my fabulous reader. I hope you all enjoy the Gold family as much as I do. I've always found my hockey teams to be a second family and I love how the boys and girls of the Gold have evolved over the books to represent that. There's nothing better than being out on the ice with your buds!

Love you all!

XOXO,

E

For Rachel S,
I see you, girl.
Thank you for always supporting my work.

GOLD HOCKEY SERIES

Blocked

Backhand

Boarding

Benched

Breakaway

Breakout

Checked

ONE

Mandy

"LESS MUGGLES, MORE MAGIC," Mandy murmured as she scrolled through her *Harry Potter* Pinterest board, trying to find the perfect themed appetizers for the movie marathon she was hosting that weekend. She knew she was unreasonably excited about having a party at her new apartment, but this was big.

As in the apartment was the biggest purchase she had ever made.

Smiling, she leaned back in her chair and continued scrolling through her phone. A hockey game was playing in the background, the volume low enough that the announcers' voices were a muted hum. But that didn't matter, she would hear if anything exciting happened, the crowd's cheers would radiate through the concrete layers of the arena to where her office was situated.

Mandy always joked that her office was Harry's equivalent of his closet bedroom—a tiny cubbyhole in the bowels of the

Gold Mine, the home rink for the NHL's newest team, the San Francisco Gold.

Her office might be small, but the physical therapy space certainly wasn't.

A half dozen treatment tables were set up in the large room outside her door, each complete with their own built-in cabinets filled to the brim with the best supplies money could buy.

The PT suite tended to be one of the hubs—players always coming in and out, lots of activity, voices, laughter—for her team, second only to the space where they relaxed, ate, played video games, or binged the latest hit on Netflix.

But for the most part, Mandy loved all the activity. She enjoyed the players crossing through to access the weight room, or take a dip in the pool, or soak their aching muscles in the hot and cold tubs. And with the team's doctor, masseuse, and other support therapy staff's own small offices surrounding hers, it was hardly ever quiet.

Except now.

While the doctor and his assistant were rink side—near the team in case anyone got injured—the rest of the training staff had gone to grab a bite. She'd stayed behind this time, nibbling on a salad and taking advantage of the mental break by blissfully scrolling through wand-shaped appetizers on her phone.

After the final buzzer, the activity would ramp up again. The players each had their own post-game routines—maybe a massage or a soak in the icy, cold tub, usually some time spent on the exercise bike, slowly cooling their muscles after the strenuous sixty-minute game.

As for her?

Her phone and those magical treats would lay forgotten because she'd be running around like a chicken without its head.

Multiple players would need different treatments, and it was her job to coordinate with the masseuse and the doctor to assess injuries old and new, advise beneficial exercises and stretches, and . . .

She spent most of her time trying to pretend that Blane was just another player.

"Idiot," she muttered as just his name conjured up all sorts of very unprofessional images into her mind.

Muscles.

The kind that made the spot just below her belly button clench with need.

Strong legs and, good gravy, but his ass.

Hockey players had the *best* asses.

No pancake bottoms, these men—and *women*—could fill out a pair of jeans. She wanted to squeeze it, to nibble it, bounce a dime—

Mandy dropped her chin to her chest, losing sight of the Sorting Hat cupcakes she'd been pondering.

Blane with his yummy ass had a unique way of distracting her.

No, it wasn't even distraction, per se. He had *always* been able to get under her skin.

And that was very, very bad for her.

"Ugh," she said, tossing her phone onto her desk and standing, knowing that she wouldn't be able to sit still now.

Nope, she needed about forty laps in the pool and a good hard fu—

Run, her mind blurted, almost yelling at the mental voice of her inner devil. *A good hard run.*

Unfortunately, the cajoling tone wasn't completely drowned out. *Some sexy horizontal time with Blane would be more fun—*

But the rest of the enticing words were lost as the roar of the crowd suddenly penetrated through the layers of concrete. Her stomach twisted. Mandy could tell, even before her eyes made it to the television, that it wasn't in celebration of a goal or a good hit either.

This was fury, a collective of outrage.

She was on her feet the moment she saw the prone form lying so still face down on the ice.

Her gut twisted when she spotted the curving line of a numeral two on the back of the player's jersey.

"Not him," she said and the words were familiar, a sentiment she had whispered, had *prayed* a thousand times before. She needed the camera angle to shift, for her to be able to see more clearly *who* was hurt. "Not him."

Then Dr. Carter was on the ice and the player moved slightly, rolling away from the camera, giving a full shot of his back and the matching twos adorning his jersey.

Fuck. Not him. Not Blane.

And that was when she saw the pool of blood.

TWO

Blane

COLD.

The ice was cold.

Some part of his brain knew that was an inane thought, even as the rest of him recoiled from the biting freeze. It burned, but not hotly.

Cold. So cold.

And quiet.

Nothing except for the whooshing sound of his breath behind his ears.

Groaning, he tried to push away from the frost, to get onto his back and away, but hands held him in place.

"Let—"

And with that one word, his mind began working fully again. The lights came into focus, the spotted mix of colors of the crowd—mostly black and gold since they were playing at home—as they stared down at him. The arena had gone remarkably quiet, seventeen thousand plus people somehow not making a sound.

A towel pressed to his forehead, and he realized for the first time that he was bleeding.

He winced.

"Blane," Dr. Carter said, and he knew his injuries must be serious if more than just Brian—the on-bench trainer—had come onto the ice.

"I'm fine," he said. "Just had my bell rung."

Dr. Carter ignored him. "We're going to roll you. Hold still while I put the collar on."

"What?"

"*Hold still.*"

Blane froze, finally understanding. He'd figured that he might have a concussion at worst, but he'd had one before, and this wasn't that. Or at least, he didn't think so. He wasn't nauseous, his ears weren't ringing, but the stern order in the doctor's voice made him realize that this could be a lot more serious than he'd first thought.

Fuck.

"Steady," Dr. Carter said, but he wasn't talking to Blane.

A collar was secured around his neck, and he was carefully rolled to his back and strapped onto a board. Then he was hoisted on top of the stretcher and further strapped in.

"Sorry I'm so heavy, boys," he joked and was relieved when the group surrounding him all smiled, albeit small ones, but they were still there. Meanwhile, Blane was trying to play it cool, trying not to panic as he attempted to move his toes.

Shit, could he?

Yes. Thank fuck.

His fingers?

A heartbeat that lasted for an eternity before he realized that yes, he could also move his fingers on both hands.

Relief poured through him.

"Let's go," Dr. Carter said after a few moments, and they began wheeling him from the ice. It was the strangest thing seeing the arena from this angle, hearing the taps of the players' sticks, the roar from the crowd, as he was being pushed out on a stretcher, unable to do anything more than give a thumbs-up.

Up off the ice and through the door leading down into the depths of the arena, focusing on the squeaking wheels of the gurney rather than the curt, whispered orders of CTs and MRIs.

He would be fine.

He was *always* fine.

And plus, he could feel his fingers, feel his toes.

He was fine.

Until he saw her.

Pale, the light brown of her eyes shimmering with moisture. She *wasn't* fine. Though she held in her tears, though her chin was lifted and her shoulders straight, Blane knew this all had to remind her of another time, another player.

She thought he didn't know, that he couldn't begin to understand.

But of course, he did.

"Stop," he snapped, half-surprised when the stretcher actually did slide to a halt. "Mandy needs to come with."

Dr. Carter hesitated for a brief second then began pushing him forward again. "Let's go, Shallows."

"But—"

"Now."

Nodding, she raced ahead of them and pushed open the arena door. An ambulance was parked outside, back panels already open. Mandy waited until they passed through then helped the stretcher into the vehicle, but when she would have hopped back out, Blane gripped her wrist with his only free body part, his fingers.

"Stay."

A long, slow breath. Her shoulders dropping just the tiniest amount.

The doors closed.

Mandy sat down next to him.

THE MRI WAS loud and Blane had a fucking headache. He'd been in the CT already and frankly felt another scan was unnecessary. But Dr. Carter had ignored him and ordered the test anyway.

"You've got a headache and neck pain, Blane," he'd said. "Yes, the CT is clear, but you still have symptoms. You know I can't leave it at that."

So Blane had shut up and acquiesced, knowing that the sooner he did, the sooner he could get the fuck out. But come on, he'd been blindsided by a six-foot-six-inch, two-hundred-and-thirty-pound player skating at full speed. *Of course* he had pain.

Hell, he'd had pain for the last decade of his career.

Something *always* hurt. That was the life—a strained muscle, a blocked shot, a stray punch to the face caught during a scuffle in front of the net.

So yeah, he was used to things hurting.

And now the magnets whooshing by his skull over and over again were making his head pound even more.

Funny how that worked.

Finally, the machine shut off and he was spit out, still wearing that damned collar. He was done, so *fucking* done that he was only a few heartbeats away from tearing that shit off.

Then Mandy stepped into the room.

And suddenly, he was as well-behaved as a schoolboy.

She had that effect on the whole team.

No nonsense but sweet as hell. Willing to always go the extra mile, to stay late, to research an obscure type of treatment in case it might help with whatever injury they were dealing with.

But recently—fine, pretty much since forever—he'd hidden something else beneath his well-behaved exterior.

Because the moment she'd walked into the room his body had exploded into awareness. His skin went sensitive, his dick—thank God *that* seemed to be working fine—twitched, and every smart, funny, brilliant thing—*ha*, perhaps not brilliant, but maybe he could have at least conjured a semi-reasonable sentence—slipped from his brain.

She was gorgeous. Incredible. Amazing.

He wanted her.

Fuck how he wanted her.

But she didn't want him.

THREE

Mandy

Mandy's heart skipped a beat at seeing Blane so still on that stretcher. It was just like—

No.

And look how that ended.

No.

"I won't bite," Blane said softly. "Couldn't even if I wanted to. They've got me trussed up like a fucking turkey."

She snorted, the terror that had frozen her in place loosening its grip. "You need to be tied up."

"Didn't think you were into kink."

The deadpan words froze her tongue instead of her brain because the images Blane conjured up with a single sentence were dangerous, oh so fucking dangerous. Trailing her hands down his body for pleasure rather than treatment, savoring the feel of him beneath her palms—hot and hard and rougher than her own skin. Forearms bulging as her fingers trailed lower, wrists straining against her bonds until . . . *snap* and it became *his* hands on her.

Sweet baby Jesus, how she *wanted* that.

And sweet baby Jesus, how disgusting was she?

The man might have a spinal injury and she was undressing him with her eyes, imagining him in bed, not focusing when she should be helping him get better.

Nothing but a disgusting little whore—

"You okay?"

Blane's question pulled her out of the words, out of another place and time, and guilt swamped her anew.

She was supposed to be taking care of him and instead she was a fucking wreck.

But she also knew how to pull herself out of that particular mindset.

God knew, she'd done it plenty of times.

So she straightened her shoulders and released a long slow breath, letting the tension, the memories, the hurts retreat back into the darker recesses of her mind.

"Sorry," Blane said just as she opened her mouth to get back on track. "I shouldn't have gone there." A hesitation. "Even as a joke."

A joke.

Here she was fantasizing about his body, about spending time in his bed.

And she was a joke.

Fucking perfect.

Mandy bent and faked tying her shoe, knowing that she was being too sensitive, knowing that she was off her game because of the hit and the potential for a spinal injury and the fact that it had been Blane bleeding out on the ice in that moment. She needed to tuck the shit away, to get her head on straight and focus.

"You don't have to apologize, Hartie," she said, gaining some distance by referring to Blane by his most recent nickname, a not very original play on his last name, Hart. "I've heard it all before."

"It was still inappropriate," he said. "I wasn't thinking."

Which made it worse. Because even instinctually he wasn't attracted to her.

So. Much. *Ugh.*

"It's fine," she said, hurrying on when he started to speak again and would have no doubt issued another flipping apology. "Should I wheel you out of here? The docs were gathered over your results a few minutes ago. No doubt they'll have some answers soon."

"Yeah." His eyes flicked over to meet hers as she grabbed on to the gurney and started pushing him out of the MRI suite. "What do they think?" he asked.

She almost made an offhand joke. The MRI was a simple precaution at this point. The concussion protocol had been administered, and Blane had passed. The CT was clear, as were the X-rays. Dr. Carter was just crossing every T and dotting every I.

But it occurred to her that Blane might not know that.

He'd been so calm and . . . himself—agreeable, steady, clear-headed—that Mandy hadn't recognized that he was holding on to some fear.

Rightfully so, of course.

The collision had been a big one, and any loss of consciousness was serious. Plus, he had a two-inch gash on his cheek that had required both internal and external sutures.

So he might seem fine, and his body might *be* fine, but that didn't mean he'd come out of this completely unscathed.

"Gabe thinks you're clear, last I heard," she said and brushed a finger over his uncut cheekbone. It wasn't unmarred, however. A huge bruise was forming, all swathes of blue and black and purple. Not pretty, but standard hockey fare. "Minus the shiner you'll be sporting for the next while."

The little wrinkle that had pulled his brows down and together smoothed out. "Yeah?" he asked, lips twitching. "So how tough does it make me look?"

She rolled her eyes. "*So* tough."

He chuckled. "That's what I thought."

The gurney squeaked as she steered it around the final corner and tucked it into the private room they'd commandeered for him.

And so now what?

They were alone—the nurses with other patients, the doctors analyzing test results. The lights were dim, only half having been switched on in deference to Blane's headache, and there was little foot traffic thanks to the Gold's security having locked down this end of the hall.

No rogue photographers would find their way in and snap a pic of him like this—immobile and helpless and incapacitated. They'd learned from before. From—

Dammit. No.

This wasn't like—

"How are the toes?" she asked and if it sounded mostly desperate, that's because she *was* desperate.

To excise the memories, to forget it had happened at all.

Blane frowned, studying her for a moment. He tried to catch her gaze, to get her eyes to meet his, but she couldn't let that happen. Mandy had a terrible poker face and her emotions always read like subtitles across her expression. There wasn't a chance she'd let them tangle with his. Not when he read too much.

"Toes are fine," he finally said after she'd spent far too long examining his stitches and the bruising on his cheek.

She nodded, all business, before smoothing several wrinkles out of the sheet covering the gurney. "And the fingers?"

Blane wiggled the digits in question. "Cooperating."

"No weakness?" she asked, checking his pulse.

"No." A pause. "Mandy."

"And the headache—?"

"*Mandy.*"

His tone made her jump, made her eyes flash to his, despite her best efforts. *Dammit.*

Her questions came rapid-fire, attempting to distract. "No headache, then? How's your pain level otherwise? Is it manageable?"

Somehow his fingers found hers. He was strapped to a stretcher, still in a collar, and his fingers managed to lace with hers.

"I'm fine, sweetheart," he said gently. "This isn't like—"

He broke off, squeezed her hand.

Tears flooded her eyes, and her throat went tight. But she couldn't cry. *She couldn't.*

"I'm fine," she said and though it sounded wobbly, at least she held back the waterworks. "*You're* fi—"

The door opened with a screech and she straightened, tugging at her fingers.

Blane didn't let them go.

Shit. Shit. *Sh*—She dropped her shoulders and left her hand in his, letting herself take this moment of comfort. She could give herself, give *him* this and still stay safe.

"Good news," Dr. Carter said as he strode into the room, the collective of other doctors on his heels. "The CT is clear. We'll take the collar off, run a few more tests, and I'll need to reevaluate you in the morning."

"Tomorrow's game?" Blane asked. "I'll be able to play, right?"

Mandy's fingers tightened. "No."

Dr. Carter walked around the gurney and gestured for her to help him with the collar. "Mandy is right. No activity for twenty-four hours minimum. You'll miss at least one game, more if you're still symptomatic."

"But I don't have a concussion—"

"At this moment, things are pointing to that," she said, removing the brace from around his neck. "Brains are tricky, yes? And you only have one, so listen to Dr. Carter and don't screw around with it."

A few coughs from the peanut gallery reminded her that she wasn't at the arena, safely ensconced in her half dozen treatment beds.

She winced. This wasn't her domain, and she shouldn't be taking over.

"Sorry," she murmured.

"No," Gabe said and he moved around the foot of the bed to give her arm a squeeze. "You're right." Together they helped Blane sit up. "Tomorrow we'll do another evaluation and go from there. That was a big collision. Minimally, you'll miss a game or two."

Mandy knew what Blane was thinking. On one hand, it was early in the season so this type of injury wouldn't necessarily be a setback to playoff hopes.

But on the other, the Gold was a young team and any time one of their veterans missed games, the whole roster suffered.

He was a critical part of their offense *and* the current leading scorer.

It wouldn't be easy to replace him.

"No negotiations," she said, stuffing a pillow behind his back. "But know you'll be of far better use to the team when you're healthy."

He sighed, frustration evident in the lines of his face. "Yeah."

"Great." Gabe snapped up the railing on the bed and stepped back. "Let me get a few things in order on the hospital side and we'll get you out of here."

Mandy followed him out of the room, eager to escape both her memories and her body's reaction to Blane. He'd been cut out of his equipment—jersey sliced, shoulder pads in pieces, hockey pants and socks shredded. The only things that had escaped unscathed were his shin guards and his gloves. But because he *had* been stripped down, he had far too much skin showing for her comfort.

What was it about Blane that made it so she couldn't distance herself? Why couldn't he just be another player?

"I'll Uber to my car at the arena," she said once they were in the hall and the rest of the doctors had gone off to take care of other patients. "Make sure everything is good there and come back to pick you up. I'm guessing you'll be done by then?"

He was glancing down at his phone, a frown on his face.

"What is it?" she asked. "Dr. Carter?"

He looked up, made a face. "Gabe," he said. "There's too much of this *Dr. Carter* nonsense going around already."

One half of her mouth tipped up. "Well, you *are* a doctor."

"Why did I hire you again?"

The familiar rapport brought her back into herself.

"Because I'm the best?"

He snorted. "True. But you should still call me Gabe."

She bumped her shoulder with his. "I *could*, except I have this thing with authority, and calling my boss by his first name is just too weird."

"*You're* weird. And a liar."

"Nailed it," she joked, tapping her nose. "Now, what's up with *that*, Gabe?" She nodded at his phone.

"Blue's down in X-ray. Possible broken hand."

"Shit."

"Yeah."

When it rained in professional sports, it tended to pour. "I'll get my car, check on the crew, and make sure Blane gets home." She pulled out her own phone and glanced at the time. "An hour to discharge him? I'll get security to send him a car."

"Thanks." He turned for the elevators then paused. "So you can't use my first name, but cursing in front of your boss is okay?"

"I'm weird." A shrug. "And it annoys you. Plus, this is hockey."

He laughed as he left, calling over his shoulder, "Make sure you sleep at some point tonight, Mandy."

"You, too, *Dr. Carter.*"

Smirking at the one-fingered salute he gave her, she headed back toward Blane's room and pushed the door open—then promptly cursed and let it slam closed.

Shit. Shit. *Shit.*

Dammit. *Fuck.*

Why hadn't she knocked?

Because now she had the image of Blane—naked, yummy, *naked* Blane burned into her brain.

And it was a fucking amazing image.

She'd already seen a lot of him, but this was . . . all of it. She had seen *everything.* And fuck, what right did he have to look so good hours after a potential career-ending collision? Mandy dropped her head against the door, fingers coming up to press against her mouth, trying to contain the mental stream of cursing to just her brain.

If one word, hell, one *sound* escaped, she was going to lose it.

She'd been pushed and pushed and *pushed.* By the memories, by her attraction. She wasn't levelheaded, wasn't remotely calm in that moment.

Nope. She was a woman on the edge and—

The door swung open.

Her arms flailed, her fingers lost their battle at containing the streak of curse words, and she toppled into Blane's room, her face on a breakaway with the hard tile floor.

But she didn't even come close to hitting.

Because Blane pulled her against his chest, steadying her against the wide expanse of smooth, hot skin and hard muscles.

And then it wasn't just with curse words that she lost her battle.

Instead, she lost her head, her body, her . . . heart.

She kissed him.

FOUR

Blane

CLEARLY HE'D HIT his head harder than he realized.

That was the only rational reason for why he was hallucinating, for why Mandy was in his arms *now* after he'd been dreaming about her for months.

But fuck it all, dream or hallucination or real life, he wasn't going to let this opportunity slip from his grip.

She was small, so much smaller than his bulky ass and so he lifted her, pinning her against the door so that her mouth could reach his more easily. Her legs wrapped around his waist and her hands came to his shoulders, pulling them even more tightly together.

Her lips were soft, her body lush, her moans—

Fuck. She was everything.

Until the hands on his shoulders began to push away instead of pull closer, until her legs dropped from his hips and scrambled for purchase on the floor, until her mouth was torn from his.

"*Blane*. Fuck. Shit. Dammit. I—"

He was hard and aching, and his headache had transformed into a dizziness he knew was less from the hit and more from the tornado that was Mandy, but when she got all flustered and started running through her repertoire of curse words, he couldn't help but want to make her feel better.

"It's okay," he said, lowering her to the ground and holding her steady as she got her feet under her. "Let's just blame the brain injury."

"I—" Her head plunked onto his chest and he took the opportunity to run his fingers through her ponytail.

Silk. Just as he'd suspected. Chocolate brown and silky and *soft*.

"I could have hurt you."

Blane scoffed. "You? Hurt me? Sweetheart, you're what, a buck ten? It's more likely my clumsy ass will crush you."

"Mandy," she muttered, talking to herself instead of answering him. "You are unbelievable." She shoved out of his arms and turned to face the door.

He stared at her rigid spine, the tense set of her shoulders.

Yes, she was. So fucking unbelievable it took his breath away.

But he'd also been around her for three seasons now, and he knew that when she was like this—stiff, tense, stubbornness radiating from every pore—that there would be nothing he could do to get through her shell.

She'd lock her armor down tight and it was strong enough to resist a nuclear blast.

Nothing would get through.

Except maybe—

"Do you think you could find me some pants?"

And there it was. She whipped around to face him. "What?"

He pointed down. "Pants."

He felt like cheering when her cheeks went pink, when her eyes drifted down to . . . well, his cup had gotten uncomfortable, so he'd taken it off. And it wasn't like there had been a towel or a hospital gown or even a suit nearby. All his gear had been cut off him except the fucking cup.

Which had been a cruelty in and of itself with Mandy popping in and out of eyeshot and making his jock go uncomfortably tight.

His fault, he knew, for making sure she'd come.

But whatever. He'd finally been untrussed, and lying there like a lump after everyone had gone wasn't going to make anything better.

So he'd gotten up in search of clothes or a gown and to get rid of the fucking cup already.

Unfortunately, he'd also given Mandy an unintentional eyeful.

After spending a lot of his life in locker rooms, nudity was just what it was. He wasn't embarrassed or shy in the least.

But when Mandy looked at him like he was a gallon of Ben and Jerry's and she was the spoon . . . yeah, he liked *that* a lot.

She coughed, eyes flicking back down and up again. He'd covered himself with his hands because he was a fucking gentleman. *Ha.* Fine. But at least he was trying, right?

"P-pants?" she asked.

He grinned.

"Yes, please. I'd like to walk out of here without creating the next Gold scandal."

"I"—she licked her lips, and his grin faded because *fuck* did he want this woman—"can find you . . . um . . . something."

He sent a mental prayer up that the *something* in question might be a bed with her naked and willing in it.

"Yeah. Uh—pants. You definitely need pants." She bit the

corner of her mouth and nodded sharply before turning back for the door and struggling with the handle.

"Hey, Mandy?"

Her chin dropped. "Yeah?"

"You kiss real good."

Not even close to proper English or even a reasonably sensible statement, but when his mind was spinning with all the dirty things he wanted to do to her at that moment, public space be damned, it was enough.

She kissed like a fucking goddess and the taste he'd had wasn't nearly enough.

"I shouldn't have done that," she said softly.

He ran a few strands of her ponytail between his fingers. "I'm really glad you did."

"It was a mistake." She pulled open the door.

"I understand."

Her eyes flew to his.

He nodded. "I won't bring it up again."

Emotions flew across her face, too fast for him to process. Gratitude maybe? And relief. But also something else. Disappointment?

Fuck. He didn't know and frankly, he was too tired and dizzy to figure it out now that the adrenaline from having Mandy in his arms was fading.

The pain was back.

He wanted to be home, relaxing on his couch with a beer.

"Bring what up?" Her lips curved just slightly and she turned back to face him, brushing her fingers across his cheek. "Sit down before you fall down. I'll be back as soon as I can and then we'll get you home."

Blane wanted to tug her close for another hit of that pure Mandy energy, but she pushed through the door and was gone before his ass hit the mattress.

FIVE

Mandy

"OH GOD," she murmured, stopping to thunk her head against the wall the moment she was around the corner from Blane's room. *"Oh my fucking God."*

She had not just done that.

She had not just opened up the can of worms that was her sexual attraction to Blane.

He had not just kissed her back.

Why had he kissed her back?

Adrenaline. Worry. A man's reaction to a highly charged situation.

That had to be it.

So why didn't it feel like that?

Why did she feel like she'd just stood on the edge of a cliff, thought *Why the fuck not?* and jumped?

She was a woman in a man's profession. She didn't fraternize with players or the team's staff, couldn't afford to fraternize, not when her contract had a clause that forbade it.

And frankly, she also didn't date within the organization because it was so cliché. Oh, girl falls for hot guy on the sports team, gives everything up for him, and lives happily ever after.

Except it didn't work out that way.

She'd lived in the product of such a happily ever after and believe her, life had not been a fucking fairy tale.

A simpering mother.

An abusive father.

Being told to be sweeter, prettier, *better* so that her dad wouldn't find fault in her, and therefore find fault in her mother. Being called ugly, stupid, useless by both parents when he inevitably *did* find fault in her.

Because he always found something that needed to be improved upon.

Except it wasn't encouraging a kid who'd missed one word on the spelling test to practice it a few times so they got it. No. Instead, it was making that kid sit down and write the word out a *hundred* times.

He hadn't scheduled some extra time on the tennis court when she lost the championship match.

He'd taken every evening, every weekend and filled them with private lessons and camps and thousands of serves and volleys and backhands.

Thank *God* she hadn't played hockey.

She had that thought every single day of her life. Thank God her dad had played in the NHL, thank God he'd been away half the year, and thank God *she* was a girl and had *no business* playing a man's sport.

And yet, she'd loved him, had wanted him to love her.

Unfortunately, sometimes people were only able to love themselves.

She'd figured that it was fate's cruel joke, her getting the job with the Gold, and she probably would have turned it down flat if it hadn't been for Gabe.

They'd met in med school, staying in touch after they'd both graduated. He'd gone on for his residency program and she'd left the field for physical therapy, completing a certification program while he'd slogged through ninety-hour weeks.

She'd quit medicine, disappointing her father one final time before he'd died.

It had been the single bravest thing she'd done, and also the stupidest . . . according to him.

But she'd never wanted to be a doctor, not in the way Gabe had. She was more interested in the body as a whole, in treating it to remove pain, to help it accomplish more.

Mandy *could* have gone into orthopedics, but she hadn't wanted to be in a hospital setting broken bones. She'd wanted to stop them from getting to that point in the first place, to get someone who had been injured back to normal, to help with chronic pain.

She wanted to fix all those things that had been unfixable in her father.

A pipe dream.

That was all it had been.

Her phone pinged, and she glanced down at the screen, saw it was her assistant. "Fuck," she said and took a breath. "Enough." After swiping a finger to answer the call, she put it up to her ear. "Hey, Callie. You guys okay?"

She listened to the rundown and was proud at how much the rest of her team had stepped up. Callie listed a few new injuries, including Blue's hand, and the treatments they'd issued. They'd done great, perfectly executing the post-game routines, and she told her assistant that before passing on the information about Blane.

"He's being discharged, actually. CT and MRI are negative,

but he'll be out a game or two, depending on how he feels over the next few days."

"That's great news," Callie said. "We were all worried after a hit like that." A beat. "They've said Player Safety will review the head contact."

"Good." She'd now watched the collision on replay several dozen times—initially attempting to distract herself from the potential for a spinal by coming up with a treatment plan for exactly how to alleviate the inevitable whiplash and muscle pain, and then afterward because some sick part of her just couldn't let it go.

As if watching again might somehow change the outcome.

Foolish.

But that aside, Blane was still waiting for some freaking pants and she had the feeling that if she didn't come back with some soon, he would start trolling the hospital halls for a pair.

At which point, Rebecca Stravokraus, the publicist for the Gold, would not be happy with Mandy, and then she wouldn't be getting her delicious recipe for brownies.

And Rebecca's brownies were the shit.

If there was one thing the women of the Gold didn't fuck around with, it was chocolate.

So no naked scandals on Mandy's watch, thank her very much.

"Look, can you send a car over for us and make sure to include some clothes for Blane—comfortable stuff, sweats and a T-shirt. Everything was cut off him, and I can't have him walking out of here bare-assed."

Callie giggled. "I mean, *you could.*"

"You, madam, are evil," Mandy said, "And a bad influence. Car. Clothes. STAT."

"Yes, Dr. Shallows."

Mandy huffed. "I'm *not* a doctor."

"You graduated," Callie said. "That's close enough."

"I'm hanging up now."

Callie giggled again. "I'll send a car."

"And clothes."

"Bye!"

"Callie," Mandy warned as the phone clicked off.

She sighed and slipped the cell into her pocket. The car had better have a pair of pants in it or so help her, she would put Callie on towel washing duty for the foreseeable future.

Her phone buzzed. She pulled it out and saw a text from her assistant.

And clothes, I promise. I don't do laundry.

Car's ETA is twenty minutes.

Mandy sighed and headed for the elevator. She might be evil, but the woman was efficient.

SIX

Blane

BLANE HAD MANAGED to bow out of the wheelchair.

Mainly because he'd walked right by it and had taken Mandy's hand, tugging her toward the elevators.

She'd brought him pants and news of the car's arrival just as he'd been dozing off.

Good thing, too.

Who knew what his dreams would be like?

A replay of the collision? Or maybe, and probably more likely, a replay of the kiss Mandy had laid on him?

Option one would have been disturbing, but option two would have been more problematic, considering his unclothed state and the thin cotton blankets. Not that the pants she'd brought were much better. He was threatening to pitch a tent from her mere proximity.

Think of unsexy things. Global warming. The exchange rate of the British pound. How the rubber of hockey pucks was vulcanized to form a precise disk that weighed exactly six ounces.

What the fuck did vulcanized mean, anyway?

He played with pucks, knew when they felt right, knew when they didn't, but he couldn't explain what vulcanized rubber was.

But he was, apparently, good at getting rid of his burgeoning boners. Look at him go, just one year past thirty and he could finally control himself.

He snorted.

Mandy glanced up. "What is it?"

"You don't want to know," he said and then pressed on before she could question him further. "How mad at me are you?"

Pale brown eyes rolled heavenward. "What would be the point?" A shrug as the doors dinged and opened and they stepped from the elevator. "I'm sure Rebecca would say it didn't look good if someone caught sight of you in the wheelchair anyway. You need to appear strong and uninjured, despite being stretchered off the ice a few hours ago."

The tone of her words—equal parts begrudging and annoyed—had him biting back a smile. "Oh yeah?"

She huffed. "Yeah."

"Rebecca's holding her brownie recipe hostage again, isn't she?"

Mandy's mouth dropped open, and she missed a step before recovering. "What the heck do you know about Rebecca's brownies?"

They stepped through the back door of the hospital. A car idled near the curb. Blane waved away the driver when he started to get out to help them.

"I know that those brownies are delicious. And that you've been trying to get the recipe for months." He grabbed at the door handle before she could, tugging it open and gesturing her inside. If his mother had taught him one thing, it was how to be a gentleman.

Even when—like now—he really didn't feel like being one.

Mandy hesitated. "You should go—"

"Sweetheart," he said, knowing he shouldn't be using the endearment, knowing it might be misconstrued as sexist or condescending, but unable to stop himself. She meant too much—

So not the time, Hart.

Not when she was scared and anxious, and he had her partway off balance.

Not when her shell had finally cracked the slightest bit.

Not when he might somehow worm his way in.

So he continued talking, knowing it was stupid and risky, but pushing on anyway. "Sweetheart," he said again, "I'm exhausted and I know you are, too. I want to be at home in my bed, passed out with late-night TV blaring in the background, and I want you to get into that car because I'm two seconds away from lifting you in myself, and I think we both know where things might end up if I get you in my arms again."

She froze for a long moment, eyes wide and staring, before she released a breath on a long, slow exhale. "*Oh.*"

"Yeah, *oh,*" he muttered, giving her a little nudge. "Now, into the car before you start regretting selling my safety for Rebecca's brownie recipe."

Mandy slid into the car and he followed. "That's not exactly fair," she protested as he closed the door.

"The truth isn't always fair."

"Where to?" the driver asked. "Back to the rink or your house?"

"We'll take Blane home first," Mandy said as he opened his

mouth to tell the driver to take her home first. She was tired and needed to rest.

"You should go fir—"

She leveled him with a glare. "Buckle up and don't argue with me, Blane. You've been through the wringer tonight. You're going home first."

His eyes met the driver's in the rearview as he buckled his seat belt. They seemed to say, "Don't look at me. I'm following her orders."

And Blane knew there wasn't any point in arguing. When Mandy got like this, she just dug in her heels and budged about as much as a mountain resisting the elements. That's to say, not much and any fractional movement had earth-shattering consequences.

The car's destination was *not* earth-shattering.

"Those brownies had better be good," he grumbled.

"What brownies?"

"The ones you're going to make me."

"Wait here," Mandy told the driver and hopped out after Blane.

They'd pulled into his driveway, a small cottage not far from where Brit and Stefan lived.

"I'm fine," he told her, pressing a few buttons on the keypad so the gate swung open. Luckily, he had another pad on his front door, since his keys were still at the rink.

"You're not—"

"I'm fine," he grumbled. "And I'm getting really fucking tired of you telling me I'm not."

"You're grumpy," she said, trailing him to the front door.

"That means you're decidedly *not* fine. You only get grumpy when you're hurt."

He input the code on the keypad, pushed the door open, and stepped inside.

"Or horny."

Her eyes went wide. "Wh-what?"

"Nothing."

So maybe she was right, maybe he was tired and hurting, but dammit, he was also horny as fuck. Which meant she needed to leave before he did something stupid.

Like haul her against his chest and kiss her senseless.

Blane plunked himself on the couch, feeling grumpier by the moment. "I'm safely ensconced like the damsel in distress you think I am, 'kay? Night, night." He closed his eyes, felt her not move from her position behind the couch.

"What?" he asked after a few moments of silence.

"Are you okay?" Her voice was hesitant, wobbling just slightly at the end.

And Blane's heart went to Jell-O.

He sighed and patted the couch cushion at his side. "I'm really okay," he said when she sat next to him. "But I don't think you are."

SEVEN

Mandy

MANDY SANK down onto the couch next to Blane. She was exhausted and vulnerable and knew it was a shit idea.

She sat down anyway.

"You scared me."

He rested his head back against the couch. "*I* scared me."

"But you were so calm."

His hand came up and tugged her ponytail lightly. "It's easy to pretend sometimes."

She dropped her head back to match his position on the couch, thinking of all the times she had pretended in her own life. "Yeah, it is."

"So you want to tell me why I scared you?"

"I care about all the guys on the team."

He moved so that his jaw rested against the fabric of the couch, his brown eyes looking almost black in the dim light. "I mean why did *I*, in particular, scare you?"

Men.

She huffed. "Blane. It was one kiss. Don't start thinking that I'm hard up for you. It was adrenaline, fearing for your life, whatever."

"I didn't mean the kiss. Though it was pretty fucking incredible, if you ask me. And"—he shrugged—"I'm definitely hard up for you. I've wanted you for months, Mandy. You're hot and capable and don't take any shit."

"I—"

His mouth curved. "Just so we're clear. But we're not talking about the kiss, remember?" He sat up enough to tap her temple. "I was referring—clumsily, I realize—to what happened with your dad."

What was the expression? All of the air had been sucked out of the room?

Yeah. That.

She turned away, swallowing hard against the memories. But it was already all so fresh in her mind, had been from the moment she'd seen Blane on the ice. "Your house is nice, *really* nice actually."

"Brit decorated it for me."

When she stood up, he followed. "Mandy—"

"I'd forgotten she'd told me about that." Her heart pounded as she pointed to the walls and inched toward the front door, the need to escape growing with every beat. "I really like the gray and yellow together. I'll have to tell her. Well"—she smacked her lips together—"I should go. You need to rest."

Blane touched her arm. "Look, obviously you don't want to talk about it and that's fine, but I get why you were so upset. I know what it must have seemed like. I just . . . I *get* it, okay?"

The tone was more insulting than the words. Hell, if she'd been feeling reasonable, both probably would have been sweet and kind.

But that was a big *if*.

Because she wasn't feeling the least bit reasonable.

She was flayed open and a fucking emotional wreck.

And Blane being all calm and all-knowing and sensible made every single one of those long-buried feelings about her father just burst right to the surface.

She shoved his arm away. "How could you possibly understand? *Hmm?*" She snapped when he stared at her in shock. "How? I've met your parents, they're fucking incredible." A laugh, broken and jagged. "My par—" She sighed and the flare of anger that had burst into flames died out rapidly, leaving only embarrassment and shame in its wake. This wasn't her. She'd vowed to *never* be like them. "Mine," she said, forcefully shoving the unreasonable outburst of emotion down. She wouldn't be like this, wouldn't explode for no reason. Not like they always had. "Mine are not."

"Sweetheart—"

"No." She took another step away from him. "I promised myself I wouldn't do this. I vowed that when I took this job, I wouldn't let them keep tearing me up like this." Her eyes filled with tears. "I *fucking* promised."

Blane took a step toward her and she raised her hands. "Don't."

He glared, closing the distance. "I'm going to hug you because you're my friend and you need a fucking hug. Just shut up and let me."

She shut up.

And he hugged her.

It was everything.

His chest was the perfect amount of firm and he was warmer than the electric blanket she cuddled under every night. But it wasn't just his body. Blane was a good hugger, holding her tightly without suffocating her, somehow knowing that she needed that much pressure in order to not fall apart.

Just like he'd known she'd needed the contact.

Somehow he knew.

How? *Why?*

"You're thinking again," he murmured. "Don't."

She laughed. "Are you a mind reader or something?"

"No." He loosened his grip and leaned back slightly. "I just know you, sweetheart."

Her breath caught.

"I know that what happened to me tonight must have reminded you of your dad, and I'm sorry for that."

Shit.

Her heart rolled over in her chest, exposed its vulnerable underside.

"Oh look, Brit picked out the perfect painting." She pointed to the pencil drawing of the Gold Mine shining brightly, the lights of San Francisco dancing around in the background. "That's one of Sara's, isn't it?"

Sara Jetty was a former professional figure skater and also a supremely talented artist, who happened to be married to Mike Stewart, one of the Gold's defensemen. The thought of Sara actually made Mandy feel a little guilty. Sara's upbringing had been tough—she'd been betrayed by both her coaches and her family—and the media shit storm that had followed was almost unthinkable.

Sara had had it way tougher than Mandy.

Which meant she needed to buck up.

Blane huffed at her obvious avoidance. "We don't have to talk about it. But I do just want to say I'm sorry it happened. I'm sorry you were hurt." He nudged her toward the front door. "Now *and* then."

She dropped her chin to her chest, equal parts won over and annoyed. "Tell me again, why do you have to be so perfect?"

He opened the front door. "It's a skill I've honed over many years."

The sound that came out of her throat was half appreciation, half disgust.

"Now, go home and get some sleep." He leaned down and whispered in her ear. "And maybe dream about that kiss." His lips brushed her skin, made her shiver. "I know I will."

Her jaw dropped open, but he simply nudged her in the direction of the car and closed the door.

She was in a fog the entire way to her apartment.

And Blane was right. She did dream about the kiss.

But she also had nightmares about all the ways that sort of kiss could go wrong.

EIGHT

Blane

BLANE WATCHED the game from a box and tried really hard to keep his expression neutral as he watched his teammates struggle on the ice below.

He knew this was the right call, not playing, but that didn't make it any easier.

He should be down there.

Fuck.

Wincing when a bolt of pain shot down his neck, he forced himself to relax and really study the boys. Maybe he couldn't play, but he could at least be useful by finding a hole in their system or something that could be used against the other team.

He'd been evaluated that morning and while his spine was fine and he wasn't showing any further signs of a concussion, his neck was seriously fucked up.

The muscles were in a permanent state of spasm, and the pain was radiating down to his shoulder. He could barely turn to the right, let alone shoot a puck or take a hit.

And he was wearing a fucking suit.

They were a necessary evil in his profession, but he still hated them. Give him shoulder pads any day of the week over a button-down and a tie moonlighting as a noose.

Okay, fine. They weren't *that* bad. But they also weren't a Gold jersey.

Especially when his team was down on the ice trying to grind out a victory against the number one squad in the league.

Not thinking, he brought a hand up to the collar of his shirt, tugging slightly to loosen his tie and then cursing under his breath when the movement made pain flare down the entire right side of his body.

"Freeze."

Mandy.

He glanced behind him and couldn't hold back his grimace. Shit. *Note to self, don't turn fast and don't move the entire right side of your body.*

"I said freeze, you big lug," she muttered. "Not move."

"Then don't sneak up on people," he grumbled.

"Cranky again." She laughed softly. "Men are such babies when it comes to pain."

"I don't want to hear the spiel about natural childbirth again." He gritted his teeth when her fingers slipped under the collar of his shirt to feel the muscles of his neck.

"It's not a spiel." Her thumb pressed hard enough for him to hiss out a curse. "It's the truth. You're just cranky that you're not playing. Now, hold still or I'll have to pull you down below for treatment and you won't be able to watch the game."

"I would just like to point out that we block one-hundred-mile-per-hour slap shots."

"And women keep having babies."

"With epidurals."

"Because we're not stupid," she countered, gripping his jaw and tilting his head one way and then the other before returning to the massage. "I also would like to think that I'd get out of the way of one of those shots. Or at least wear some of those thick ass pads that Brit has."

They both paused and watched Brit line herself up to block a puck on the ice, holding their breath against the booming sound it made when connecting with her shin guards.

She popped back up and made another save, this time covering the puck for a whistle.

Mandy glanced at him, shook her head. "Goalies."

"Now *they're* the crazy ones."

She grinned. "I'll agree with you on that." Her fingers drifted a little lower. "Your shoulder is hurting, too."

Blane went to shrug and winced.

"That's a yes," she said. "I can't work on it here without giving the fans a show, so make sure you see me after the game."

"I don't want to take time away from the boys."

Her eyes flicked to his, narrowed. "And *I* don't want you to miss any more games than you have to."

The crowd erupted as Mike picked an opposing player, sending him neatly over his shoulder when the young gun didn't keep his head up. The kid took it well, popping back to his feet and joining the play as the Gold took the puck down to the opposite end of the ice.

Stefan snuck in down low, avoiding the player guarding him, and got off a nice shot their goalie stopped and held on to.

The ref blew his whistle and the red light came on, signaling a TV time-out. A replay of Mike's maneuver began streaming on the Jumbotron, and the ice crew came out, running their shovels across the surface to collect the snow that had been created from both teams.

Coach huddled the team close and was drawing something on his whiteboard.

Blane sighed. "I'll come down."

"I know you want to get back out there." Mandy rested her hand on his shoulder. "I want you there, too."

His lips twitched. "You just want to get rid of me."

Her mouth followed suit. "Maybe."

She turned for the door, pausing when he called, "Mandy?"

"Yeah?"

"I thought you were avoiding me."

She'd practically hidden in her office the entire time he'd been down in the PT suite, popping her head out periodically when Dr. Carter called out a question but generally keeping her distance.

He'd known why. He'd pushed her too far the previous evening, after she'd already been shoved clean out of her comfort zone.

But dammit, he'd expected something that morning.

A softening to the distance she kept with everyone, for him to be . . . fuck, was his mind *really* going there?

He wanted to be special.

Barf.

He'd never given two shits about being special before. He wasn't one of the best players in the league, though he worked hard and put up good numbers.

But he wasn't an all-star like Brit and Stefan, and he was fine with that.

He earned his place. He'd had a long career.

That was all he had ever dreamed of.

And he'd spent so much time focusing on hockey, fantasizing about a relationship that would have never, *ever* worked out, pretending it wasn't the right time yet, that he couldn't risk her career—

Yes, he'd been in love with Brit for half his life.

She'd lived in his house for several years when they'd both been teenagers playing junior hockey. Blond, lithe, and beautiful, Brit also had a huge heart and was incredibly down-to-earth, and the entire team had crushes on her. But she'd friend-zoned him from the beginning and with her living in his house, it wasn't like he could hit on his "surrogate sister."

So friends. He'd figured he could live with that until they were older, until things changed.

Except, things hadn't changed and Blane had finally realized that what he'd imaged as true love wasn't that. Of course he *loved* Brit, wanted her to be happy, and he'd also loved the idea of having his best friend as the person who completed his life.

But then she'd found Stefan, and Blane had realized she could have never completed him.

He needed to complete himself.

Look at him being so healthy and shit.

Mandy's chuckle pulled him out of his head, her words further so. "I *was* avoiding you this morning."

He hadn't expected her to admit it so readily.

"Evals come with a ton of paperwork," she said with a dismissive wave of her hand.

Blane pushed out of the chair and crossed over to her. "Really?" he asked. "That's how you're going to play this?"

Her smile stayed fixed in place, but her eyes went sad, and that loss of spark hit him right in the gut. "That's how I've got to play it, Blane. This job is all I have, and I c-can't— I'm sorry. I just can't."

He forced his tone to go light, to curve his mouth up into some semblance of a grin. "Well, the good thing is that I know all about coming in second to a career, so at least there's that." He turned back for the game. "I'll see you later."

"Blane," she whispered, but he didn't face her, just strode

over to his chair and determinedly watched the game. "I'm sorry."

"It's fine," he said and felt her hesitate before she left.

Second best. Yeah. That was a familiar feeling.

NINE

Mandy

MANDY WENT BACK to hiding in her office. Which was where she should have stayed in the first place.

Idiot.

She'd seen Blane wince one time on the live broadcast before the camera had cut back to the players on the ice and she'd all but run upstairs to the box he was watching the game from.

He was hurting. She needed to save him.

Ha.

She needed to run. To keep her distance because the dream last night had been too good, because the memories were too real, because his kiss had made her stupid.

Her kiss, she reminded herself. She was the cause of all this trouble. She'd started it and so she was the one who needed to finish it. Which meant she had to force her relationship with Blane back into the strictly professional, if slightly friendly, box from which it had burst.

Her contract forbade fraternizing with the team. She knew that. He knew that. Some quick sex wasn't worth losing her job or the inevitable tension that would come when their interlude came to an end.

No matter that the kiss had blown every single one of her previous sexual fantasies out of the water.

The man's mouth and tongue were better than any penis—

Okay. She was getting off track.

The point being, this job was important to her and she couldn't risk it. Also, there was the fact that Blane would soon be under contract negotiations because this was the last year of his current deal. He was older, and this was probably his final chance at a really good contract.

How could she possibly risk that for a couple of orgasms?

She couldn't.

Groaning, she dropped her head onto her desk. Then there was the fact that he played hockey. The risk that he might turn out like her father.

Wouldn't that be the real mindfuck in this whole played-out scenario?

If she somehow ended up just like her mother. Unhappily tied, never measuring up, lonely.

Except Blane wasn't like that.

She sighed and lifted her head, rolling out her shoulders before reaching for the salad she'd packed for dinner.

"That green stuff will kill you," Blane said from the open door behind her.

Mandy jumped and the container flew from her hands, landing on the floor. Luckily, the lid stayed on. "So will stalkers who sneak up on people.

"I knocked," he said. "You were too busy groaning to hear it." He grinned. "I'd be groaning, too, if I had to eat that."

She shook her head. "You do *have* to eat it. This is straight from the nutritionist handbook."

Blane wrinkled his nose, and Mandy's heart pulsed. The man was way too cute for his own good. "I like PR-Rebecca better."

"Nutritionist-Rebecca has you all playing better than ever."

A shrug. "PR-Rebecca has brownies."

"I know. Now I've got you thinking about those chocolate squares of deliciousness, too, huh?" Mandy grinned when he gave her a sad look and nodded. "They're like two sides of a very evil coin. One will torture you with veggies and the other will fatten you up with baked goods."

"It's true."

"So?" Mandy asked when he didn't say anything further. "What brings you down to the dungeon earlier than ordered?"

Blane started to shrug then froze and clenched his jaw. "Figured you'd be busy after the game. Thought you might want to get me out of the way now so you don't have to stay late."

Mandy had wanted him to come by after the game because the PT suite was currently empty, the other staff off to grab dinner, Gabe and company on the bench. This was her quiet time, but this was also a dangerous time for Blane to be there because they were alone.

But she couldn't tell *him* that.

Not when she was trying to shove him firmly back into the friend zone.

Friends didn't worry about being alone with each other.

"Never mind," he said when she didn't move. "I don't want to interrupt your dinner."

He turned to leave, and Mandy noticed the stiff set of his shoulders, the tilt of his head. Immediately, guilt filled her. He hadn't come down to get her alone or to disrupt her meal.

He'd come because he was hurting.

Not that one of her stubborn hockey players would ever admit that. They might be babies when it came to shots and deep tissue massage, but they were still "tough" and didn't like to show any sign of weakness.

And she'd been about to leave Blane suffering because she was having difficulty separating her attraction to him.

Nice.

She pushed to her feet. "Are you kidding? I'm looking for any excuse to not eat the damned stuff. Come on." She slipped by him and patted the nearest table. "Shirt off, hop up."

Opening the drawer, she surveyed the contents then began pulling out what she'd need and stacking it on the tray next to her.

She rotated to face him after she'd finished, mentally preparing herself for the visceral shock that always came when seeing Blane without a shirt. What she wasn't prepared for was for him to still be wearing one *or* for him to be struggling with his tie.

"Damn," he muttered before dropping his hands and tilting his head to stretch his neck.

He didn't look at her as he began fumbling with his buttons, biting back a curse every time he lifted his right arm.

"Stop," she ordered, thinking that someone out in the universe must really hate her. "I'll do it."

This would not affect her. He was a patient. Nothing more.

Lies.

Every last one of those was a fucking lie.

Because when she walked around the table and stood before him, it didn't matter that they were currently standing in a huge room blazing with fluorescent lights. The space shrank and darkened, until it was as intimate as if she were undressing him in a candlelit bedroom.

Blane's breath caught when her hands came to his tie. "I'll come back—"

"I've got it." And despite everything, her voice was husky, her pulse thundering.

Slowly, she slipped one end of silk free from its knot and tugged it from the collar of his shirt. It fell, landing soundlessly on the floor. She reached for the buttons—

"Don't." His hand caught hers.

"Ignore it," she murmured. "Please, just ignore it."

A nod, his teeth so tightly clenched that she could hear them grinding in the near soundless room.

Her fingers fumbled with the first button, struggling to push it through the little oval hole in the cotton for a long moment before she managed. They both released breaths when that first inch of skin was exposed. The space behind her navel quivered in need and her thighs trembled, but she ignored her body and reached for the next button.

This one was easier. It slipped free and more of his chest was in her view.

Another shoring breath, another button, another inch of skin.

She could do this. She was a fucking professional.

But then she undid the last fastening and spread his shirt wide.

Her breathing was rapid, her hands shaking but still she pressed on, carefully helping him slip the cotton from his shoulders.

Oh, fuck.

So much skin. Her mouth watered, dying to taste, to run her tongue along the hard plans of his chest, down around the squares of his abdomen.

She sounded like she'd run a fucking marathon, and she

might as well have with as much as her body ached to go to him, to rub herself against him, to slip his pants—

"Shit," she hissed and slammed her eyes closed.

He was hard.

And not his chest.

Fingers cramping, palms itching, she forced herself to turn back to the table. "Up you go."

"Sorry," he muttered, sitting down and putting his shirt over his lap.

"Happens," she lied. Because it didn't fucking happen.

Or very rarely anyway. And definitely not from just taking a shirt off. Maybe during a thigh massage, but she usually was able to dissuade any funny business because though a thigh massage might sound like a good idea to a few of the young ones, the older players knew it wasn't comfortable. Frankly, it bordered on painful, and that was typically enough of a mood killer, young or old.

Blane lay down and closed his eyes, his lips moving in a way that looked like counting.

"What are you doing?"

"Thinking about player stats," he gritted out.

She frowned. "Why?"

"Because I have a fucking boner and I'm trying to get it to go away."

Her hands froze, the bottle of topical pain relief lotion six inches from his shoulder. "Oh."

"Yeah," he muttered. "*Oh.*"

Mandy bit her lip, tried to stop the sound from escaping. It didn't work.

Blane's eyes flashed open, darkened to espresso by a combination of irritation and attraction. "Are you seriously laughing right now?"

"Uh-uh." She shook her head, chest still shuddering from stifling her giggles. "Nope."

"Oh, my God," he groaned. "You are. I'm in pain over here and you're cracking up about it."

Her amusement faded and she quickly opened the bottle. "Shit, Blane. I'm so sorry. I shouldn't have—" Moving rapidly, she spread the lotion onto his neck and shoulder. "That was wrong of me."

His left hand came up to stay her wrist. "That's not the pain I was referring to."

Heat flashed across her cheekbones. "Oh."

He rolled his eyes. "You and your *ohs*."

She snorted.

"You're laughing again."

"It's a ridiculous situation." She began massaging the pain cream into the knotted muscles of his neck and shoulder. "Flip over," she told him. "This will be easier from behind."

One brown brow rose and her cheeks flared hotter.

"Shut up, you."

"I'm not the one who's doing all the sweet-talking."

She motioned for him to turn. "Lips. Zipped. Roll onto your stomach and we'll kill two birds with one stone. Erection gone"—she made a popping sound with her lips—"and I'll be able to get some of the knots out. You have spasms all over."

Blane shifted so that he was facedown. "That's not the only place I have—"

Mandy gently, but persistently forced his face down into the table. "Don't finish that sentence."

His shoulders shook in silent laughter, but thankfully his sentence remained unfinished and finally, she got down to real work. Some basic massage since that wasn't her specialty—they had a full-time masseuse on staff for that—but it loosened the muscles enough for her to help him with some stretches. Then came the TENS machine, followed by ultrasound.

By the time the final buzzer for the game sounded, Blane's muscles were relaxed and he was snoring on the table.

Erection to snoozing. Yeah, she was totally irresistible.

Twenty minutes later most of the players had finished with the press and began filtering into the PT suite.

"You killed him," Brit teased, coming over.

"It's a gift." Mandy shrugged. "But seriously, I doubt he got a good night's sleep with all that muscle pain."

"Yeah." Brit sat on the next table over, her finicky shoulder already on full display. She winced when Mandy set an ice pack onto the offending limb then flicked her gaze toward Blane. "So when's the wedding?"

Mandy's eyes shot over to Blane's snoring form before lobbying a quelling glare at her friend. "Brit," she warned.

"What?" Blue eyes widened innocently. "You guys are perfect for each other. You know I've been telling you that for months."

Mandy sighed. "And I've been telling *you* that I have no interest in a relationship right now. This isn't the time, not with my plans to expand my role here, to focus more on keeping the team healthy."

"It's not that I don't want us healthy," Brit said and wrapped her fingers around Mandy's wrist. "It's just—"

"That you want me to be happy." She pulled free, bopped her friend on her good shoulder. "And I thank you for that, but—"

"You're too scared to take a chance." A piercing look. "Work is a convenient excuse."

"It's not an excuse." Okay. Or not much of one.

Brit's expression said that she saw through that lie.

"Look," Mandy said. "I've dated around some since I've

been in San Francisco. The schedule is too much to build something serious. I'm gone more than I'm here for half the year and even when I'm in town, the days are long." She shrugged. "And I'm not one for a casual fling."

"Which is perfect." Brit clapped her hands. "Blane doesn't do casual. You shouldn't worry about him and me, you know. He never looked at me the way he looks at you."

Her breath caught. "How does he look at me?"

Brit grinned. "Like he wants to get you alone in the PT suite and bend you over one of these tables."

"Oh, my God," Mandy said, her eyes shooting to Blane—who thankfully snored on—and then around the room to make sure that no one was in hearing distance. "You did *not* just say that."

An unrepentant shrug. "So what if I did. It's true, and plus Stefan and I—"

"La. La. La." Mandy covered her ears.

Brit pulled one hand off. "Seriously though, if you ever decide that it's the right time, give him a chance okay? He's solid. And attractive, if you like the built, super sexy but sweet athletic type."

"Brit," Mandy sighed.

"Okay, fine," her friend said. "I'll leave it alone. For now."

Considering that Brit had been bringing up Mandy dating Blane like clockwork every few weeks for the last six months, she knew that her friend's *for now* really meant *for now*.

"So he's not hurt too badly, right?" Brit asked as Mandy helped her stretch out her shoulder.

"No. It was a lucky thing that he ended up with just muscle pain."

Brit nodded. "Yeah, lucky for sure. I don't like seeing any of the guys get hurt, but it was especially bad to see him. He's like my brother."

Mandy paused, helped Brit move to another stretch. "I get that."

"He's always just seemed so infallible, you know? Like, he's my best friend, Stefan aside of course, but I mean, I've known Blane practically forever, and I don't think I've ever seen him stay down." She shrugged, dislodging Mandy's hands. "It just reminds you that everyone's place in this game is fleeting, you know? It can be lost"—she snapped her fingers —"like that."

Mandy knew that. Viscerally. Had experienced it in her own family.

"I just . . . it's—"

"Shut up, Brit." Blane turned his head toward them.

Brit grimaced. "Shit. Sorry, Blane. I was talking loudly again, huh?" She bit her lip. "I didn't mean to wake you up."

He slowly rolled to his back and pushed to sitting. Mandy moved to help him, and neither of them clued Brit in to the fact that she had not, in fact, been talking loudly. Rather, Blane had been saving Mandy. Again.

Saving her from rehashing in her mind the fact that her father had been paralyzed on the ice from a hit very similar to Blane's.

That he hadn't been okay.

That he'd been plagued with health problems until his death.

That the paralysis had left him angry and hurtful.

Well, he'd *always* been that way. Being unable to play hockey had just ramped up the volume on each and every one of his horrible characteristics.

But she didn't really want to get into that with Brit, not when mentioning her father always brought around the same lamentable reactions. First, before his injury, her dad had been a great PR perk for the NHL—he'd been good-looking, charming, the perfect exceptionally talented but down-to-earth family man.

Which just basically meant that he'd hid his abuse and affairs really well.

He'd been popular enough to have big advertisers with primetime commercials. He even had a movie cameo or two.

And on the ice, he'd been well on his way to smashing scoring records.

Then the hit came.

He'd put on a good show afterward, broadcasting a bit, keeping himself in the public eye, until health complications had made even that impossible.

Which was the point when it got *really* bad at home.

She'd been fifteen, old enough to understand a bit of what he lost, but still young enough to want his approval and love.

It was not meant to be.

No matter how hard she tried or how many A's she brought home or serves she hit.

Approval from her father was not to be had.

But Blane didn't know any of that. He'd just made the connection that she, Mandy Shallows was the only daughter of Roger Shallows, former NHL great to most, but drunken, abusive asshole of a father to her.

"How's the neck?" she asked softly.

"Better." He squeezed her hand as Stefan came over to talk to Brit, then he leaned close to ask. "You okay?"

She slapped a little more pain-relieving gel on his neck. "You need to stop worrying about me. You've already got enough on your plate."

He shook his head. "I don't think that's possible." A beat. "Have dinner with me tomorrow."

Mandy straightened. "You know I can't."

"It's easy," he said. "You just say three letters."

"A. B. C." She sighed when his face fell. "You know there are a lot more than three reasons for me to say no."

"I *don't* know," he said and stood. "But I get that this is probably not the time or place for this discussion."

Her shoulders relaxed when she realized he wasn't going to push. But there was also a drawback to him being so intuitive and thoughtful, and it wasn't one she wanted to admit, not when some of the armor that she held so tightly around her heart was weakening.

Hell, it might as well be cheesecloth when it came to Blane.

"Hey!" Brit called. "I wanted to ask if Blane could come on Saturday. Stefan can't make it, and Blane is more into HP than Stefan anyway."

Mandy glared at Brit. So much for leaving it alone. Her friend just shrugged as if to say, *"It's later."* Sighing, Mandy turned back to Blane, expecting him to give her another out.

That wasn't to be, however.

His lips curved into a smirk. "What's Saturday?"

"*Harry Potter* marathon!" Brit said, one hand taking the ice pack Mandy shoved back at her, the other waving an imaginary wand. "Come on, do it! Blane might know more random movie and book trivia than I do, and that's saying something."

"Oh." Her eyes flicked to his. "Really?"

He pointed to his chest. "Nerd central. I love the little lightning-scarred dude. I can't help it."

Stefan snorted.

Blane extended his finger—not the pointer one this time—in Stefan's direction. "You, my crazy American, don't know what good literature is."

"Hey," Brit said. "*I'm* American."

"Well, you lived in Canada with me long enough to be an honorary Canadian."

"Also, your mom is American, dude." Stefan pulled his

phone from his pocket. "And I think that she needs to know that you think Canada is better."

Since this was a typical argument-slash-chirp-slash-threat between Blane and Stefan, Mandy and Brit ignored them for the time being.

"You going to be up for it?" Mandy asked. "We could reschedule—"

"Are you kidding?" Brit exclaimed. "I'm dying to see how you decorated my old apartment. The pictures of the floors looked incredible. I bet the space looks so much bigger now."

Mandy couldn't stop herself from smiling, even though she felt slightly embarrassed, as though she were bragging, when the only reason she'd been able to afford the apartment at all— student loans were a big ol' bitch—was because Brit had cut her a spectacular deal.

"It looks good. Brit—"

"You're not allowed to thank me again," her friend said. "I needed to get rid of the apartment, and you needed somewhere permanent to stay."

"I guess. But—"

"Wingardium leviosa."

Mandy frowned.

Brit shrugged, dislodging the ice pack. "I panicked," she said. "Couldn't think of the spell to stop someone from talking."

Mandy paused, wracking her brain.

There *had* to be such a spell and further that, it was probably very obvious.

"Damn," she said after a moment. "I can't believe it, but I don't know it either."

Blane broke away from his argument with Stefan long enough to say, "I think the spell you're looking for is *Silencio.*"

Her gaze flicked to Brit's, who grinned. "Told you he was good."

"*That* I know," she muttered.

"So?" Brit asked after Mandy had strapped the TENS machine to her shoulder. "Is he in?"

"Yes." Blane had come behind her and his mouth was very close to her ear. "Is he *in*?"

She shuddered, turning to face him . . . or rather to glare at him because the tone of his question had been decidedly wicked, and he knew it. Of course, he knew it. She pressed her fingers to her cheeks, attempting to will away her blush. "You can co—"

Come.

Mandy had been about to say come.

The fucker saw right through her hesitation, too.

Except how could she finish the sentence now?

Thus far, he'd managed to turn way too many of her sentences from something innocuous into something very dirty.

He would definitely do that if she told him he could come. Or in. Or—

Got it.

"You're invited," she said triumphantly.

"Yes!" Brit fist-pumped as Blane merely smiled, his eyes amused.

"Looking forward to it." A wave to Brit and Stefan. "See you all tomorrow." He brushed his fingers across hers before walking out of the PT suite.

Mandy couldn't help but feel like a piece of her heart went with him.

TEN

Blane

THANKS TO MANDY, his neck pain was near to nonexistent the following morning and he practically skipped into his follow-up evaluation with Dr. Carter.

"Much better, Blane," the doctor said. "So long as you stay symptom-free, I'll clear you to play on Friday."

Which meant he would miss another game, but considering the alternative—that arguing with Dr. Carter tended to get players more time off the ice than on it—Blane clamped his jaw closed and accepted the doctor's orders.

He had just sat on a stationary bike when he spotted Mandy walking into the PT suite.

Fuck, but she was beautiful.

There was something about a woman who was comfortable enough to wear T-shirts and sweatpants, her hair pulled back into a ponytail that spoke of a certain confidence.

Don't get him wrong. He'd loved women in all shapes, sizes, and colors, dressed up or down or in between.

But women in athletic wear—and yoga pants in particular—were hot.

Or maybe that was just Mandy.

He had the feeling that she could be wearing a plastic garbage bag and she would still be the most beautiful woman in the world to him.

So yeah, he had it bad.

Now what to do about it?

She was into him, that much seemed obvious, but it wasn't like he could push her. This was where they worked and attraction or not, he couldn't risk making her uncomfortable.

So what?

Wait around for her to make the first move?

It had taken her close to three years to kiss him.

He shook his head and started peddling, acutely aware that while they'd worked together for three years and while he'd thought her pretty and competent from the get-go, he'd been nursing a broken heart for much of that time. It had only really been the last six months that he'd been obsessing over her.

Despite her grumbling from the evening before, she loved salads, though she never put dressing on them, the weirdo.

She was, obviously, super into *Harry Potter*.

Her favorite color was orange and she had a pair of bright orange sun-shaped earrings that she wore when she was feeling really happy.

Her eyes were brown, but they were more—milk chocolate with streaks of dark and gold.

So no, he didn't think he had another six months' worth of patience in him.

And he was right back at square one. How was he going to convince her that—jobs aside—he was worth taking a chance on?

The door swung open, and Brit and Stefan strolled in. Blane

quickly tore his eyes from Mandy and focused his gaze on the screen in front of him that was counting miles and calories.

"We missed you at our run this morning," Brit said, claiming the bike next to him.

"I don't think my body can take another beating at this point," he said.

Brit's marathon sprints up and down the arena stairs were as legendary as they were brutal . . . and the woman simply flew. His best hope was just not to be left too far behind.

"True," she said, blowing on her nails and mock-buffing them on her shoulder. "You're slower than a tortoise."

He shook his head. "You need to work on your chirps."

"I know. I'm hopeless." Her nose wrinkled. "So did Doc clear you for tomorrow?"

Blane made a face. "No. But Friday, as long as things are good."

Stefan had stopped for towels, and he reached across Blane to hand one to Brit before taking the bike on the other side of him. "Don't rush it."

"I'm fine." Blane peddled a little faster, feeling a bit like the filling of a very talented sandwich. "I'm getting better every day."

"I agree with Stefan," Brit said, hanging up the towel and starting to move on her own bike. "The season's young. We'll need you more later on."

"Yes." Stefan nodded. "Exactly what she said."

"Right." Brit flashed a smile at her boyfriend. "And those are the words every woman dreams of hearing."

He blew her a kiss. "I love you."

"I know you do." A nod that made Brit's blond ponytail fly forward.

Since Blane was feeling like a seesaw trying to keep up with the couple's banter on either side of him, he kept his eyes forward and satisfied himself by simply rolling his eyes. "You two are disgusting. You know that, right?"

Brit reached over and threatened to press a button on his screen. He batted her hand away and then froze.

The pedal hit him in the back of the leg. "Is that—?"

She bit back a smile and nodded.

A year ago, he would have expected to feel bittersweet, perhaps a little sad. But all Blane felt in this moment was joy. His best friend was happy, and that was all that mattered.

"Congratulations," he said, jumping off his bike to pull her into a hug.

"Careful," Brit warned. "Don't hurt yourself."

"Shut it." He folded her in his arms, smelling the familiar floral scent of her shampoo. "I'm so happy for you, Peanut."

"You realize that I have way more embarrassing material on you than a bad nickname, right?"

"Damn right, you do." He stepped back. "But seriously"—he shook Stefan's hand before punching him on the shoulder—"It's about time that you made an honest woman out of her."

Brit rolled her eyes.

"I'm kidding," he said. "I'm happy for you both." When her expression clouded slightly, he asked, "You okay?"

"I think I should probably ask *you* that. Is this"—she pointed between the three of them—"all right?"

He snorted. "It's about three years too late to be asking that question."

"Blane!"

He tugged on the end of her ponytail. "I'm fine. I promise," he added when it looked as though she would protest. "I'm happy if you're happy."

"Good." She wrapped her arms around him for a quick squeeze. "Now, get your ass back onto that bike so you can be in shape to backcheck for me on Friday."

"So bossy," he joked as he returned to his bike.

"I think you mean, so right," she said.

Mandy popped her head in at that moment. A few of the guys were behind her and they all wore curious expressions. "I saw hugging. What's wrong?"

"This." Brit held up her hand, showing off the giant diamond that had first caught Blane's eye.

Mandy squealed. There was no other word for it. She turned to Stefan. "You did it!"

He gave a little shrug.

"About time." She pushed into the room and hugged Brit. "I'm so happy for you guys."

The rest of the team piled into the weight room, filling the space with congratulations and gentle ribbing.

"Brit will poke her eye out with that," Mike Stewart, Stefan's D partner, joked.

Blue, his hand still wrapped but thankfully not broken, asked innocently, "Do you even have any money from that big contract left? That ring could feed a small nation."

"*Finally* you're going to make an honest man out of him, Brit," Max, another defenseman and a total kid at heart, complete with an obsession with video games and figurines, teased.

Blane slipped to the side, looking on with a smile on his face. Brit and Stefan's happiness was a palpable force in the room.

"All right, all right," Brit finally said after a few more minutes. "Let's get back to work, people."

Blane crossed over to her acting like he was going to give her another hug . . . but instead moved quickly to grab her head and put her in a headlock. He messed up her hair before letting her go. "Yes, boss."

She pointed her finger at him, hair tumbling all over her face. "So. Much Trouble."

He saluted. "Sic Dan"—her brother who was currently working as an FBI agent—"on me if you want. But, somehow, I think he'd approve."

Grumbling, she fixed her hair and got onto her bike. "You're lucky I love you."

"You're lucky *I* love *you*," he countered then called to the room at large. "Dinner at my place tonight to celebrate these two jokers."

She glared. "It had better be your pasta."

"As if I know how to cook anything else."

Her lips twitched. "True," she said, her words halting for a few seconds as she began peddling through a difficult stretch of the program. "But I'll tell you why *you're* the lucky one when it comes to me loving you."

His own pulse was speeding up as he got down to work. "Why?" he puffed.

"Because of this—Mandy!" she shouted before the object of his fascination could slip out the door. "You're coming to Blane's tonight, right? You told me earlier that you didn't have plans, and you're definitely invited." She nudged Blane with her elbow and he nodded.

Mandy's cheeks were bright red. "I should leave you guys to it."

Which was exactly the wrong thing to say in front of a group of players who were in such good shape largely because of her efforts in the training suite.

The room was filled with urgings for her to come from all sides.

After a few seconds, she caved like a cheap suitcase. "Okay, okay. I'll be there," she declared before leaving the room.

Brit flicked her eyes to his. "*That* is why."

"You're an evil genius."

A flash of white teeth. "Don't you forget it."

ELEVEN

Mandy

WHAT IN THE hell was she doing?

Well, technically, she was standing on the front porch of Blane's house, an engagement gift in one hand, a bottle of wine in the other, but the mental chastising wasn't because of her gift choice or her decision of red wine over white.

Nope. She was trying to find some distance from Blane, and here she found herself at his house.

Again.

What makes an idiot for two thousand, if you please, Alex.

Then a picture of her face would flash onto the screen.

She wasn't going to come, had actually planned to beg off with a headache, until Brit had texted with a picture of *her* beautiful face pulled into a hangdog expression.

Don't flake, please.

You're as much a part of this team as I am.

Come. Please.

So Mandy had come.

And now she couldn't reach the doorbell or the handle. But just as she'd almost resorted to knocking with her skull, the panel of wood swung open and she was face-to-face with Blane.

Or rather face-to-*back*, because he wasn't looking forward. "I'll just grab it from my car—"

"Uh—*oof.*"

"Wh—*shit.*" His hands came up to her shoulders, steadying her. "Sorry, sweetheart, didn't see you there."

Warmth radiated from his fingertips down through the light jacket she wore, through the T-shirt underneath, straight into her skin. It swirled below the surface, shooting sparks out her own fingertips, making them itch with the need to touch. That heat slid down her chest, her stomach, *lower.*

So much need from such a simple touch.

"You okay?" he asked. "I didn't hurt you, right?"

She cleared her throat. "Nope. I'm fine." She held up her full hands. "I come bearing gifts."

His smile stole her breath. "I'm glad you're here."

Words wouldn't come. She wanted to reply that she was glad, too, but instead all the desire for Blane was twisted up with fear and a need to keep herself safe.

He seemed to realize that fact.

"Go on in." He nudged her shoulder gently. "The crew is mostly here. I just need to grab my bag from my car."

Mischievousness was rampant in his last sentence.

She plunked her hands, gift and wine bottle and all, onto her hips. "And what's in that bag?"

A grin. "News articles."

Mandy raised a brow. "What about?"

"Stefan's removal from a few of the most eligible bachelor lists."

A *few*? Ha. Not likely. Still, these were hockey players, and they could take a little ribbing as easily as they gave it out.

"How soon until Brit guts you?" she asked, stepping inside.

He strode out onto the porch. "Probably from page one."

She laughed, walking past the couch where she'd sat with Blane only the night before and following the sound of voices. They eventually led her into a stunning kitchen.

Gray cabinets, white countertops, a turquoise backsplash. The space could have been straight out of an HGTV show. And that was all she saw because about ten of the guys were gathered around the huge kitchen island, beers or glasses of wine in their hands. They turned almost as one when she walked in, and then she was surrounded in a sea of greetings and fist bumps.

Brit emerged from behind them, a spoon in her hand. "Try this," she said and practically shoved it in Mandy's mouth. "Isn't it good?"

It *was* delicious, in fact, and probably both the reason the kitchen smelled so good and also why the guys hadn't strayed far.

They were probably desperate for a meal that wasn't approved by Nutritionist-Rebecca.

"It *is* really good," she agreed and handed Brit the gift bag. "Here."

"What is this?" Brit asked.

Mandy set the bottle of wine on the counter. "Just a little something."

She'd bought the pairs of matching cozy socks a few weeks ago, after Stefan had secretly shown her the options for rings he'd been considering, because one, they were cozy socks and no one could go wrong with cozy socks, and two, they'd made her laugh, emblazoned as they were with "Do these socks make me look engaged?" Then, en route to Blane's house, she'd stopped at their favorite restaurant on the Peninsula and bought a gift card to round out the silly gift.

"Stefan!" Brit called, clapping her hands. "Presents!"

The guys dutifully stopped talking and watched as Brit opened the present.

"The pink pair is for Stefan," Mandy quipped.

He snagged them and held the socks up by his ankle, modeling. "Pink is definitely my color." He winked, before setting them carefully next to the gift certificate Brit had pulled out. "Thank you for this"—he hugged her—"and your help with the ring."

Mandy shrugged. "Of course."

"You knew?" Brit gave her squinty eyes.

Mandy brushed them off. "*Of course,* I knew."

"Why didn't you tell me?"

She tapped her chin, pretending to stare up at the ceiling in intense thought. "Because it's *supposed* to be a surprise."

Brit wrinkled her nose. "I *hate* surprises."

"Lies," said Mike as he walked into the kitchen with his wife, Sara, in tow. "Sorry, we're late." The guys turned to greet him.

Stefan tilted Brit's chin up to press a quick kiss to her lips. "He's right. You love surprises."

Brit crossed her arms. "Maybe," she conceded, flashing Mandy a smile before going over to hug Sara and Mike

"You're a good friend."

Mandy didn't jump. She'd felt Blane come into the room a few minutes before, her body intrinsically in tune with his presence.

Danger. Danger.

But in that moment, with her friend so happy, with her little surrogate family around her, she couldn't force the armor back up around herself. These were people she trusted, people who trusted her.

She just wanted to relax and not be on edge.

"She's easy to be friends with," Mandy said, smiling up at Blane. "But then again, you already know that."

"I've got my half of the *Best Friends* necklace already, don't try to steal it."

She laughed. "I wouldn't dare." A pause. "Do you still wear it now that she has Stefan?"

"Every night when I cry myself to sleep."

Mandy snorted. "You're ridiculous."

"And you're beautiful," he said, making the air hitch in her lungs. "Now, go on." He nodded in the direction of Sara and Brit, who had been joined by their friend Monique. "Enjoy yourself tonight."

Blane slipped back to the stove, stirring a massive pot of sauce, and something inside her tightened further, the tension ramping up so tightly that it threatened to break.

She forced herself to head over to Brit, Sara, and Monique.

Instead of letting her last thread of control snap and launching herself into Blane's arms.

Enjoy herself.

Yeah, she had a few ideas about that.

Sighing, she forced the *ideas* out of her brain and joined in on the conversation.

"I can't believe your drawings are going to be at the de Young," Monique was saying to Sara.

"What?" Mandy asked. "Sorry to interrupt, but that's amazing!"

Sara glanced down, biting back a smile. "I know. I mean, I shouldn't say that because it sounds super braggy, but I'm so, *so* excited."

Brit put her arm around Sara's shoulders. "You're allowed to be excited. You've worked hard."

Sara blew out a breath. "You're right. I did."

"Can we all go to the opening together?" Monique asked. "I'll call up some friends"—she was a former model with designer *friends*—"and get us all dresses."

Brit wrinkled her nose.

Monique crossed her arms. "It's either this or wedding dress shopping."

Brit made a fake vomiting sound.

"It'll be both," Mandy said, shooting Brit a glance. "You know Monique is the only one we trust with this sort of thing."

"Is she?" But Brit was smiling. "Look at you, all gleeful over there. You've been trying to get me into one of your designer dresses for months."

"That's because your body is incredible, girlfriend."

Brit rolled her eyes. "I acquiesce to your dress up skills. For these two events *only*," she hurried to add when Monique's face went from pleading to ecstatic to overjoyed in the span of a microsecond.

"No take-backs!" Monique decreed and they all burst into laughter.

Mandy grinned. "Watch out, Brit, pretty soon you'll have hired yourself a full-time stylist."

Brit stopped laughing. "And now we can't be friends anymore."

"I've worked on you in PT for years—you should know I'm impervious to threats by now."

Sara cackled. "Owned. And anyway, I don't see why you're so against clothes. Like Monique said, your body is incredible, but I'm sure it's hard to buy something off the rack. It might be easier to let someone dress you properly."

"Properly?" Brit huffed. "I have T-shirts and sweats. I'm covered."

Monique rolled her eyes. "You're hopeless sometimes, you know that, right?"

"The last time you tried to get me to wear something it had ruffles!"

Mandy chuckled as the conversation went on, loving the banter between her friends, the inside jokes and funny references. She about died of laughter after they'd all eaten their fill of the delicious pasta and were gathered in small pockets in the living room, and Blane produced the laminated news articles and tweets lamenting the fact that Stefan—and also Brit—were now officially off the market.

"I haven't married him, yet," Brit grumbled, but her expression was amused.

"True," Stefan said, holding up a sheet. "This woman says if I marry her instead, she'll get my face tattooed on her—"

Brit snatched the sheet. "So. Much. Trouble."

Stefan grinned then kissed her softly on her jaw. "I only want you," he whispered, softly enough that he'd meant it just for Brit's ears. Mandy had been sitting on the couch next to them, but now stood and slipped away, wanting to give them their privacy. "It's only ever been you."

Her heart clenched, and if she were being truthful, she was jealous.

She wanted that.

Eyes drifting away from the happy couple, her gaze landed on Blane.

He was watching her, his brown eyes warm. Hopeful.

She wanted *him*.

TWELVE

Blane

HIS HOUSE HAD CLEARED OUT. Only Brit, Stefan, and Mandy were still sitting on his couch. The girls were laughing over some scene from the most recent episode of *Real Housewives* while he and Stefan were discussing the latest from Pierre, Stefan's father and also the current owner of the Gold.

Blane hadn't been joking about becoming the latest Gold scandal. In the four short years of the team's existence, they had first weathered sexual assault allegations—the player in question having been rightfully fired and found guilty after a trial—then they had hired Brit, the first female player in the league. After which, the GM had been fired and the board completely dismantled when they'd attempted to extort Brit. That didn't even include the firestorm of Brit and Stefan's romance or Mike dating Sara Jetty, the former disgraced—but now reinstated—gold medalist and the media furor that had ignited because of it.

Walking pantsless out of hospital probably wouldn't have

even made anyone's radar after all that, but Blane figured he should help PR-Rebecca out as much as possible.

Especially if he wanted her to make brownies.

"I don't want to like him," Stefan muttered after telling Blane how his father had taken his mother on a trip that summer. "But he makes my mom happy."

Which was said with about as much enthusiasm as Blane felt when he was eating off Nutritionist-Rebecca's meal plan.

"Well then you have to suck it up," Blane said. "He's good for the team."

"I guess." He stood. "Ready to go, babe? We should let Blane get his house back."

Brit nodded. "Yes, we should. I'm tired and you have that *thing* in the morning"—she shot Blane a look that made it clear there was no *thing*—"oh, but before you go, Mandy," she said when Mandy stood as well. "You should have Blane give you the name of his cabinet guy. I know you were thinking about redoing them in the apartment, and his are really nice."

Mandy's brows drew down and together. "I—"

Brit strode over to the kitchen and yanked open a drawer. "Show her the soft-close slides. They can't slam. *Show her*."

"This has to be the most pathetic thing I've ever witnessed," Blane muttered under his breath.

Stefan snorted before crossing over to Brit and grabbing her arm. "We'll let you show Mandy your *drawers*. Later, Blane."

Brit gave him a thumbs-up as Stefan hustled her out.

Neither he nor Mandy moved as the front door opened and closed.

Then she shook her head and picked up her purse. "I know she's my friend, but that woman is about as sly as a two-ton bull in a china shop."

"I would agree with you."

She played with the strap of her bag and addressed the

elephant—or bull, rather—in the room. "Brit has apparently decided we'd be good together."

"I don't think she could have made her feelings any more obvious if she tried."

She nodded. "I should go."

"I'll walk you out," he said and began heading toward the front door. "I can bring the name of the cabinet guy in tomorrow if you really do want it. He did a good job."

"Soft-close drawers?"

"You know it."

She touched his shoulder. "I do want to replace them, so I'd appreciate it. Thanks."

"No problem."

They both hesitated by the closed door.

Finally, he released a breath. "God. This conversation is the worst."

Her laugh was relieved. "It is seriously the worst."

"I don't exactly know how to save it," he said and then internally rolled his eyes. *Smooth, Hart. Real Smooth.*

"I—" She broke off with a sigh.

"You what?"

"I can't lose my job, Blane," she said, stepping back, eyes glittering with tears. "It's all I have."

"Why would you lose your job, sweetheart?"

She huffed, turning away for a second before rotating back to face him. "It's in my contract, Blane. It's in yours. Fraternizing between the staff and players results in job loss for me and a fine for you."

"That's not—"

"And furthermore, your contract is up at the end of this year. You can't afford to look bad, not when it's possibly your last chance at a really big deal before you retire—"

Whoa. Retirement? He was, hopefully, years away from considering that.

"And if you get mixed up with me, sooner or later someone will realize who my dad is, and I can't—*I can't* pretend that he was all great and good and expound to the media about him."

Her chest rose and fell in rapid movements.

"Sweetheart," he said, placing his hands carefully on her shoulders. "First, you would never have to talk to the media if you didn't want to—"

"I'm sure PR-Rebecca would say different—"

"Never," he repeated, waiting until her gaze met his, until she saw he meant it. "Second, my contract is *my* worry. I've been doing this for a long time now, and I know how things go. I trust my agent to do his best for me."

"But—"

"No buts." He brought his fingers up to brush her cheek. "And retirement isn't something that is remotely on my plate—"

She frowned. "It needs to be."

"My 401K is in good shape. That's the only thing that really matters."

"What if you don't get another—" She broke off.

"Contract?" he asked. Her nod made him shrug. "If I don't get another offer, I'll figure it out. I always do, but I can't worry about it here and now, or I'd never be able to focus on playing. It'll work out, it always does."

She sighed and stepped away. "Except when it doesn't."

"What's this really about then?" When she didn't answer, Blane braced himself, a sinking sensation gripping his inside. "Are y-you not feeling what I'm feeling?"

Silence. Then . . .

"No."

Well fuck, that didn't feel great at all. He grabbed the door handle.

"I feel more." Mandy's shoulders dropped. "I feel *so* much more. It's crazy and it's not even really anything yet, but I'm drawn to you. More than any other guy. Ever."

He took a breath, releasing the handle. "If that's the case, then why aren't we going for it?"

"Because of our jobs—"

"That's not it," he said. "So let's just retire that excuse here and now."

"It's not an excuse—"

He fixed her with a look. "Brit and Stephan are dating, are *engaged* for fuck's sake. *You know* we could go and talk to Pierre, run it by him and find a way to make this work if there really is a future between us. But you're too scared." He bent, eyes locking onto hers. "And you know it."

"So what?" she said, exasperation in every syllable. "Normal people are scared about this kind of stuff. Normal people don't feel—"

"That's bullshit, and you know it. Normal people fall in love all the time."

Mandy plunked her hands on her hips. "Well then, maybe I'm *not* normal."

"You aren't," he said, brushing his knuckles down her cheek. "You're special, sweetheart, and I want to give this thing between us a chance. I want to find out if we're *it* for each other."

She took a step toward him, close enough that he could feel the heat of her against his clothes, that her breasts brushed his chest when she sucked in a breath. "I—"

One more centimeter.

She only needed to move one more centimeter.

God, it would be so fucking easy to close that last little bit of distance between them, to haul her close and kiss her, to strip off every stitch of clothing and worship her with his mouth.

But he knew deep down that if he pushed her in this moment . . .

He *couldn't* push. He'd break something deep inside their relationship, something that had hardly formed.

And so he waited and hoped.

And then he swallowed his disappointment.

"I can't," she whispered, hands reaching behind her as she scrabbled for the handle.

He closed his eyes and shored himself up then pushed her hands to the side and opened the door for her. "See you around, Mandy."

She didn't spare him a single glance back, just fled for her car.

THIRTEEN

Mandy

She was a grown woman. An adult. She was responsible, even occasionally sensible.

So why did she feel like she'd just made the biggest mistake of her life?

Sighing, Mandy plunked her head down onto her steering wheel while stopped for a red light. It was the right call, the *safe* choice, to end things with Blane before they even got started.

This way neither of them would get hurt.

Except . . . it *already* hurt.

She lifted her head just as the light turned green, and as she drove to her apartment, she tried desperately to hold on to the belief that she'd just saved herself and Blane a lot of heartache.

"Ah, *fuck*," she groaned and before she could second-guess any further, slid her car into the right lane and executed a quick turn.

She had to go back.

She had to jump on this chance with Blane.

She had to risk it.

Except, as soon as she completed the turn, her stomach knotted and all of those second thoughts drifted right back into her brain.

"Dammit!" She punched the steering wheel but stopped herself from completing the loop that would put her back in the direction of Blane's house. Instead, she continued forward and then made a left at the next signal.

No. Home.

It didn't matter that the action made her a weakling who was afraid to take a risk.

At least she would be a safe weakling.

"Ugh!" She stopped at another signal, warring with herself. "You're pathetic, you know that, right?" She asked her reflection in the rearview mirror.

How was she nearly thirty-years-old and this pathetic?

Disgusting.

She made a right turn.

And lasted a block before she went left.

Shit. At this rate, she'd be home next week.

Her phone rang, trilling through the hands-free system on her car. The number was one she didn't recognize—which normally would have gotten the offending caller an immediate ignore and block, but tonight she jumped at the opportunity for distraction. Maybe they'd try to sell her a timeshare in Hawaii.

Maybe she'd buy one.

Hitting the button to accept, she waited for the call to connect then said, "Hello?"

"Is there a reason you're taking the labyrinth tour of the city this evening?" Blane asked.

"What?" Her eyes flicked to the rearview, to the car stopped behind her at the red light. "Are you *following* me?"

"Maybe."

"But *why?*"

She heard more than saw his shrug. "I was worried about you after you left. You were upset."

Understatement of the night, she'd been a wreck and not because of Blane, but because of her own hang-ups and all the shit that went along with them. She'd left home more than a decade before, been on her own for a long time. Why wasn't she over her childhood already?

"I'm fine," she whispered, accelerating when the light turned green.

Blane trailed her. "Yeah. Somehow I knew you'd say that."

Another signal, but this time it didn't change on her, and she cruised through with his car still behind hers.

"I'm a grown woman," she said, half trying to convince herself and half wanting to hear what he'd say in response. "I can take care of myself."

"I know you can." A beat before his voice dropped and went a little husky. "And I know you are. Hell, sweetheart, I can still feel the imprint of your ass on my palms, your tongue against mine. Fuck, I've been dreaming about the way your body felt since that kiss."

She turned left again then stopped right before the entrance to the underground garage for her building. "Uhh . . ." Fuck, why couldn't she admit to him that she was feeling the same way?

He cleared his throat. "Well, I'm glad you're home safe. I'll see you tomorrow."

He signaled, readying to pull around her, and she almost let him go, but then some inner force gripped her tightly and shook her hard.

She could *not* let this moment pass.

Mandy might be able to run from a lot of things, but she couldn't live with running from this.

This was Blane. He'd followed her home, not expecting anything, after they'd argued. He wasn't mad that they didn't agree, wasn't punishing her over and over again. He was understanding, supportive. He—

"I have a guest spot."

The signal stayed on, but his car didn't move. "Mandy?"

"It's yours if you want it," she said. "For tonight, it can be yours."

"And if I want it for more than just tonight?"

Her throat tightened, fear in every cell. "I don't know if I can give that much."

Silence.

Pulse pounding beneath her skin, tears stinging her eyes, she let off the brake—

"I'll take whatever you're willing to give."

"Oh." Her breath shuddered out.

"Turn, sweetheart," he said gently. "I'm hanging up now."

The phone clicked off, and she was acutely aware of Blane's headlights as he followed her car down. She pressed the button on her remote to let herself in then waited on the other side of the gate to do the same for his car.

Two minutes later, she was in her spot and Blane had parked next to her.

A knock on her window made her jump.

Mandy cracked her door.

"I can go, baby," he said. "Right now. No consequences, no expectations. It's *okay*."

The words were enough.

Because he truly meant them.

Because her situation wasn't the same as her parents'.

Because it was about time that she finally started living her life for *her*.

Not for them. Not for him.

For her.

She grabbed her purse and opened the car door enough to slip out. "Stay," she said. "Stay for me."

His hand came up to cup her cheek. "Always."

Sliding his free hand into hers, he waited for her to close and lock her door then let her lead them to the elevators. She slid her card over the sensor then hit the button for the sixth floor. Less than sixty seconds later, she'd unlocked her apartment.

"You sur—"

Mandy didn't let him finish the question, just rose on tiptoe and pressed her mouth to his.

That was enough.

The door closed, the dead bolt slammed home, and then his hands were under her thighs, urging her higher, coaxing her legs to wrap around his waist.

And his mouth . . . good God, his mouth.

It was against hers, teasing and demanding in equal measures, his tongue slipping between her lips, urging hers to tangle with his. Every bit of banked desire she'd been suppressing over the last months roared to life with the speed of a raging brush fire.

One second all was good. The next she was burning up.

He took a step and stopped and that was all it took for her mind to flare to attention.

She tried to slip from his arms. "Oh God, Blane. Your neck. I've hurt you."

"*No.*"

His sharp tone snapped her out of her panic immediately. "Then what?"

"First—" His lips, slightly reddened and swollen from her mouth, twitched into a self-deprecating smile. "I've wanted you for so long that I'm trying not to blow my load like a teenager."

She relaxed, attempted to suppress her own grin. "Is there a second statement to go with the first?"

"Yes." His mouth dropped to hers again, urgent and hot and dizzying. "But I'm a grown man." His kissed the tip of her nose. "Problem solved."

"Problem solved what?"

"I remembered where the bedroom was."

"*Oh.*"

"God, I can't wait for you to make that sound when I'm inside of you."

Her mouth dropped open.

"Can't resist that," Blane said, and then his lips were against hers and he was carrying her across the room and through the door that led to her bedroom.

Her back hit the mattress a moment later, and he broke the kiss long enough to lean back and say, "If you need to stop at any point, just say the word." His chocolate eyes locked with hers. "At *any* point, sweetheart."

She put her hand on his chest, just above his heart. His pulse pounded against her palm. "Thank you." She gripped at the fabric. "But for now, less talking, more kissing."

He ripped off his shirt, reached for the hem of hers, his expression almost predatory.

"*That* I can do."

FOURTEEN

Blane

BLANE SLID Mandy's shirt up and over her head, stopping only to toss it to the floor and toe off his shoes before reaching down to unzip the hot-as-hell knee-high boots she wore.

He almost told her that next time she needed to wear them and nothing else.

But there might not be a next time.

Fuck.

He couldn't think that. Not this time. Not now when he wanted to savor every single moment.

Her jeans came next and then she was in her bra and underwear before him.

Not lace, not some fancy see-through push-up number.

No, this was cotton and comfort and yet somehow still intrinsically female. In other words, it was purely Mandy.

"You're beautiful," he said when her hands hitched as though she were fighting the urge to cover herself. "Perfect."

She snorted. "Not hardly."

He kissed her cheek. "This is the time to accept all compliments gracefully. You do it for me, sweetheart."

"I—*mmm.*"

Her retort transformed into a moan and her fingers slid into his hair as he trailed his tongue along her jaw, stopping in the space just behind her ear. Filing away her reaction, he whispered, "I've dreamed about you for ages."

Her breath hitched and gooseflesh rose on her skin.

"Wait—" she protested as he made his way down her throat, but then he'd pushed her bra aside and sucked one nipple into his mouth. "*Blane.*"

A quick movement and he'd unhooked her bra, tossing it to the side somewhere in the vicinity of her shirt. Then both breasts were free. He didn't know where to go first, to her nipples—hard and ready for his mouth—or to her mouth, swollen and calling for more of his kisses.

Or lower.

Mandy made the decision for him, leaning up to slant her lips across his for a hot, drugging kiss before gripping his hair tightly and shoving his head toward her breasts.

His neck twinged slightly at the movement, but then her fingers were on the ache almost before it registered, massaging away the slight pain.

"Sorry," she panted. "I'm sor—"

He flicked his tongue across one nipple, using his free hand to tweak her other, not wanting anything to pull her out of this moment. If he only had this one shot, then he was damned well going to take advantage of it.

"Oh, God," she groaned as he sucked on her nipple, teasing it with his teeth, using his tongue to tease her until she was writhing beneath him.

And then he switched sides.

Her fingers were in his hair, tugging, straining as he brought her higher, until her hips were rubbing against his and he could barely see, so strong was his need to be inside her.

Trailing his mouth lower, he kissed across her abdomen, the outside of each hip, the top of her pelvis. Then he was sliding her underwear down as he made his way toward the hot, wet center of her.

The first touch of his tongue against her pussy made her scream.

"Blane. Please!"

His cock went impossibly harder, his fingers clenched into fists, every muscle in his body went ramrod hard. He licked her again, forcing his hands to relax so that he could spread her wide and slip his tongue through her folds.

She was absolutely dripping and the best thing he'd ever tasted.

One thumb teased her entrance then slipped inside as he kissed her clit, learning what she liked, finding the rhythm that had her grinding against his mouth and crying out his name as she exploded.

"Fuck," she said. Her breaths came in rapid exhales. "That was—"

"You're incredible," he said, grabbing his shirt to wipe off his mouth.

"Hey." She cupped his jaw. "You stole my line."

Blane's cock was threatening to crack in half, he was so hard, but somehow she made him smile. He was also probably two pumps away from embarrassing himself, so when Mandy trailed her hand down his chest, heading in the direction of the button of his jeans, he captured her palm and brought it to his mouth.

"I need a minute," he said.

She hitched one leg around his hip. "And I need you inside me."

"I want to make it—"

"No expectations, remember?" She rolled to her side, stretching for the drawer of her nightstand and pulling out a string of condoms from inside. "This is just us. This moment. And we have all night."

While Blane liked the sound of *all night*, he also knew that he wasn't about to come like a schoolboy after two strokes, his woman needing more.

Not going to happen.

So he grabbed the condoms from her hand and stuck them near her head. Then he proceeded to use every single trick in his arsenal in order to make Mandy insane with desire again. He kissed along her jaw to that spot behind her ear, he sucked on her nipples, slipped his hand between her thighs, rubbing her clit until she was moaning his name again.

And then, only then, did he allow himself to tear off his jeans and put on a condom.

She was gorgeous, her creamy skin flushed pink with desire, her eyes hazy with need, her thighs spread, her pussy glistening.

Fuck, did he want her.

But he also wanted to keep her.

"Now," she demanded, grabbing for his cock and positioning it by her entrance.

When he hesitated, trying to find just a little more control, she shattered every last thread of it by thrusting her hips up and taking him inside.

"Fuck," they both hissed.

His forehead dropped to hers, and he concentrated on just breathing, just trying to hold on.

"I need you to move," she said. "*Now*."

She flexed her hips against his, and he was gone.

He moved deep and fast and she urged him on, meeting him

thrust for thrust, her head writhing back and forth on the pillow, her eyes shut tight, her muscles straining for . . .

Then, *thank fuck*, she exploded a heartbeat before his own release rose up and swallowed him whole.

He came to cradling her against his chest, both their hearts still thundering, sweat coating their bodies.

"I knew it was going to be good," she whispered. "I just didn't realize *how* good."

Blane held her close, knowing that this was the type of *good* he would never want to give up.

FIFTEEN

Mandy

MANDY SHOT AWAKE AROUND SIX, heart pounding. She pressed her hand to her chest for a second, trying to figure out why she felt so off.

Oh.

Because she was alone.

Her bed was empty, the side that Blane had slept on cold.

"It's for the best," she murmured. How many times had she told him that it was only for the one night? He'd obviously listened.

That was a good thing.

Sighing, she slid from beneath the covers and stood.

Ouch.

Every single muscle in her body was sore. In a good way. In the *best* way. But . . . she wanted more.

And *this* was why she didn't make rash decisions late at night, while feeling emotional about her past. Blane had given her a string of the best orgasms of her life as they'd worked their way through her stash of condoms, but she'd also opened up a part of herself to him, and she didn't know how that was going to work out.

Would it be awkward at work?

Would he just jump to the next girl?

No. That wasn't fair. Blane wasn't one of the guys on the team who dated anything with a pulse. He was steady and solid. He focused on the game.

But what if he wasn't interested in her any longer? What if he'd gotten his fill and was done?

What if she wanted more?

Because, dammit, she kind of did.

He'd held her tightly the night before, resting his chin on her head, each of their heartbeats slowing, their breathing returning to normal.

The contact had felt . . . nice.

Ugh. No, that wasn't the right word. It was just that her job was filled with contact, with touch. But it was always *her* touching the players and honestly, often times she was putting them through some discomfort in order to get them back into fighting shape.

They didn't touch her.

Which was probably a good thing and spoke of a healthy work environment.

But sometimes days would go by before she realized that she hadn't had a single "normal" touch—a hug, a fist bump, a brush of someone's fingers against her arm.

And it had been years since she'd been held by a man.

Plus, if she was continuing with this honesty thing, she'd never been held like how Blane had held her, never felt safe and important and valuable.

He'd made her feel that way.

So it was just perfect that'd she woken up and found herself alone.

She walked naked to her bathroom and pushed open the door. Then promptly shrieked and whirled around.

Apparently she *wasn't* alone. Steam curled around the room, caressing her skin in hot damp tendrils. The sound of the shower was obvious, now that she was actually paying attention.

She'd walked in on Blane naked. Again.

Heat teased her spine. Fingers brushed down her nape. "You're making this a habit." He kissed the spot behind her ear, the one that never failed to make her shiver. "Though"—he trailed calloused fingertips down her arms then forward to cup her breasts—"I like this version of you bursting in on me better."

Mandy's gaze drifted down and her stomach clenched at the site of Blane's big hands cupping her breasts. "I'm sorry," she breathed as his thumb traced over the hard peaks of her nipples. "I didn't realize . . ."

He tugged her closer, until his chest pressed against her back, until the hardness of his erection nudged at her bottom. "I'm an early riser."

She snorted.

"You're as bad as some of the guys." He chuckled. "I didn't mean it that way," he said, half-scolding, though amusement was ripe in his tone. "I was going to run out and surprise you with breakfast."

Aw.

A blip sounded in her brain, reminding her that this man was dangerous, but she ignored it as she turned in his embrace. "What would you have gotten me?"

"Chocolate croissant and a dirty chai latte."

Her lips curved. One, because that was her exact order and two, because watching his mouth form the word "dirty" was a treat in itself.

"You know my order?"

He shrugged. "I pay attention."

"Mmm." She rubbed her nose against his throat, loving the way he smelled, the way the stubble of his unshaven jaw caught her hair. "Well, how about we get breakfast later?"

"Yeah?" he asked, hand coming up to cup her nape. He hissed out a breath when she nipped his neck. "What could we possibly do now?"

She leaned back, waggled her eyebrows. "I may have a few ideas."

"We should probably get to them before the hot water runs out."

"I have a tankless water heater."

He grinned. "God, I love it when you talk dirty to me."

"Soft-close drawers," she whispered, her own smile impossible to contain. "*Farmhouse* sink."

"Fuck, you're hot."

She burst out laughing. "I like you, Blane Hart."

He scooped her up in his arms. "Good. Because I like you, too, Mandy Shallows." One brow came up. "Now tell me that you have more condoms."

"What will you give me for them?"

"How about an orgasm?"

"Make it a double."

He rolled his eyes. "Greedy."

"I just know my man."

Blane froze and she realized her slipup, but instead of letting her talk herself into a full-on panic, he just kissed her until her brain turned to mush, until she was concentrating so hard on trying to catch her breath that she couldn't have summoned a frantic thought to save her life.

"Condoms?" he asked when he eventually broke away, both of them breathing hard.

She pointed to the cabinet and he used his free hand to open the drawer and pull out a packet.

"Orgasms now," he said, stepping into the shower with her. "Dirty chai's later."

"Why does that sound like the title to a bad porn film?"

He set her on her feet, testing the temperature before nudging her into the hot water. "If you're still able to make snarky comments, then I'm clearly not doing my job right."

"I'm always able to make snarky—"

His lips came down on hers, hard and demanding.

She broke away after a minute, pulse pounding, breath coming in short staccato puffs. "See. It's impossible to stop. Sarcasm is just part of my—*oh*."

His hand slipped between her thighs, and she forgot all about snark and sarcasm and witty one-liners.

"I swear to God," he said, dropping to his knees and tossing one of her legs over his shoulder, "you making that noise is the sexiest sound in the universe."

Her hips tilted toward his mouth, so close that she could feel his hot breath mere centimeters away from where she wanted it.

"See if you can make me make it again."

A smirk as he closed the distance between them and flicked his tongue over her clit.

For the record, Mandy made the sound.

More than once.

SIXTEEN

Blane

IT FELT FUCKING incredible to be back on the ice again.

Blane ran through his usual pregame warm-up—skating two circles around their half of the ice, a brief stretch along the boards, a few shots to help Brit focus and to loosen up his arms.

The buzzer blew, and they cleared off the rink to let the Zambonis come out to clean the ice.

This was the time that some coaches would come in with last minute comments and things to watch out for, but Coach Bernard didn't work that way. He'd said everything he wanted to say earlier in the day and, instead, left them to their own devices, which usually meant Frankie came in to talk to Brit, and Stefan gave some sort of motivational speech that was punctuated by bad jokes from Max.

"We should watch the—"

"Latest episode of *The Bachelor*," Max interjected with a cheeky grin. "You would *not* believe who he gave a rose to. I mean, Celina is just such a bitch."

Stefan was well-used to the interruptions by now and he'd confided in Blane that he actually thought the casualness in the locker room in these moments relaxed everyone so they played their best hockey.

Not that there wasn't something to be said for being focused and intense.

But there were times that too much tension made them cautious, everyone holding their sticks too tight and afraid to make a mistake.

And Max actually had *some* self-control. He didn't usually make asinine comments when Stefan was really trying to make a point.

"How many women are left?" Stefan asked, proving that he was a good captain. "Six?"

"Four!" Brit chimed in as Frankie left.

Mike shook his head in disgust.

"Shut it, you." Brit pointed at him. "Sara told me that you watch—"

Mike chucked his glove at her. "You're not allowed to talk to my wife anymore."

"Oooh!" Max clapped his hands together. "Dish, Brit. Now."

"Children," Stefan said, interrupting them before they could really get going. "It's fifteen minutes until game time. Can we focus?"

Brit and Max made faces, but they both shut their mouths as Stefan went over a few last points and by the time he'd finished, the guys were dressed in dry gear and ready to play.

Brit led them back to the ice.

The crowd roared as they strode into view, lights flashing, music blaring as the team took a few quick laps and then settled onto their bench, the starting lineup at the blue line and facing the flags.

As always when he played, the anthem was a total blur. A few quick notes and then he was readying himself to take the first face-off of the game.

A short blare of a whistle, jockeying to get his stick in the best position to win the puck back to Stefan, and then . . .

The ref opened his hand.

The introduction of composite sticks—rather than wood— meant that the sound of his and his opponent's sticks colliding didn't sound like it used to. Instead of a *crack* or a *snap*, they almost made a zipping noise as he battled for the puck.

But neither the fight nor the sound actually lasted more than a fraction of a second.

Wait. Wait. Wait. A breath. Then go, go, *go!*

Blane won the puck back to Stefan, and his team was off.

A pass to Mike, who flicked it up the boards to Blue. Over the line and into the offensive zone. A blocked shot that Blane managed to recover and send over to his other winger, Trent. Another attempted shot that was deflected up and out to the netting for a whistle.

And that fast the first shift was over.

Blane skated to the bench less than thirty seconds after he'd started, feeling winded and exhilarated all at once.

The offensive coach tapped him on the back as he snagged a towel to wipe his visor.

"Nice start."

He nodded in response, handing the towel back to one of the trainers and squirting some water into his mouth before refocusing on the game.

The second line was struggling to get the puck out of their defensive zone, and Brit had to make two really strong saves in a row in order to stop them from being down barely a minute into the first period.

Finally, they got the puck out and hurried for a change. The third line jumped onto the ice and spent half a minute in the other team's end before returning for the fourth line to take their turn.

Then Blane was on again and skating hard with the puck down the right side of the ice.

He saw the skater coming for him and dodged, turning enough that the hit only grazed him and he slipped by, managed to get a pass to Blue's stick, who pulled off some sort of dipsy-do maneuver around the defense Blane could have never hoped to make.

Blue broke toward the net, made another deke, and . . . was picked.

Just that quickly, play moved back into their zone.

Back and forth, sprint up, sprint back, shoot, pass, hustle, work, breathe *hard* in between whistles.

Again. And again. And again.

The period ended in a tie.

A quick chat from Bernard, a few pointers as they tore off wet underclothes, skates, and gloves and swapped them for dry ones.

Then they were back on the ice for the second period and the third.

More hits, more face-offs, more battles along the boards for free space in front of the net—

The puck found its way to his stick and he shoved it home.

Fuck, yeah.

Blue rushed over and hugged him. Stefan, Mike, and Trent following suit as they skated for the bench.

They were now in the lead with two minutes left.

Blue nudged him on the bench, a smirk on his face. "I do all the hard work and you steal my goal?"

Blane grinned. "Better lucky than good sometimes."

"Don't you know it."

Blane squirted him with water, but they were both laughing. The young one wasn't so young anymore, and he'd gotten good with a snarky comment.

They both focused on the game then jumped on the ice when Bernard wanted them out there instead of the fourth line. The opposing team pulled their goalie and added a sixth skater, making it a struggle to get out of their own end.

But eventually they did, Blue managing to scoop the puck up just past the red line and carrying it down for an empty net goal.

They skated back to the bench, relieved to have the cushion of the extra point.

"See," Blane said. "I've left the easy ones for you."

Blue snorted and shook his head.

A few minutes later—Brit having not needed that second goal because she'd secured her shutout—both teams skated off the ice and headed for their locker rooms.

Media first. Then showers and the PT suite for those who needed it, the pools or the weight room for those whose routine demanded it.

Dr. Carter had wanted to give Blane one final check after the game, so freshly showered, he headed that way.

Well, he would have gone there anyway, but Doc had given him a pretty excuse.

Mandy had been avoiding him again. Well, they'd had the best fucking shower sex of his life, followed by a breakfast filled with their usual joking and banter. But then they'd both gone to work and when he'd texted her after practice yesterday, she'd ignored him.

Then had given him a wide berth that morning.

And even now, she wouldn't look at him. She'd glanced up when he'd walked into the room and then quickly looked away, focusing on Blue's hand.

The disappointment that had been festering since the previous evening grew.

Sighing, he submitted to the stretches and exam that Mandy's assistant—even that made him grumpy since usually she would have looked at him herself—put him through and then waited as Doc looked over his paperwork.

"All's good, Blane," Dr. Carter declared not much later.

"Thanks, Doc."

Doc nodded, hesitating for a moment before indicating the table at the end of the row. "You should probably wait for Mandy to check you out though."

"Wh—"

Blane's protest cut off when he saw the look on Doc's face.

"She likes you, Blane." He sighed. "And she never likes anyone. Don't give up now. Go for it."

Blane glanced around, dropped his voice. "I'm not giving up, but it's kind of hard to go for something when it's all one-sided."

"If it were all one-sided, she wouldn't be avoiding you."

"You noticed that?"

Dr. Carter shrugged. "Kind of hard to miss the sexy eyes you two keep throwing at each other."

Sexy eyes? Blane ignored that for the moment. "She has barely looked at me."

Doc pointed to the TV screen and Blane squinted, relief pouring over him when he saw that her gaze was fixed on the two of them.

"She's good at hiding," Doc said. "But not that good. You just need to know when to look."

Blane sighed. "That's not all. She's worried about her job."

Dr. Carter's face went hard. "You going to fuck her over?"

"*No.* Of course not, but I don't want to hurt her either." Blane shoved a hand through his hair. "She's scared, fucking petrified, no matter what I say—" He blew out another breath. "And frankly, I don't know how to get through her walls."

Doc nodded. "I've known Mandy since med school, so I can tell you this: she's never looked at anyone the way she looks at you." He rolled his eyes. "Part of me can't believe that we're even having this conversation. But, we are, and dude, she's into you."

Blane flicked his gaze over his shoulder, watched as she examined Blue's hand. She was beautiful, capable, and a puzzle he'd yet to completely solve. "Maybe," he said, slanting Dr. Carter a rueful look. "But how in the hell am I going to get her to take a risk on us?"

Doc clapped him on the shoulder. "I'm guessing she's going to make that leap herself." A beat, his eyes flicking to the reflection again. "Just be patient. She'll come around." He lowered his voice. "And talk to Pierre for fuck's sake. Take that fear away for her, at least."

"I wi—"

"Blane?" Mandy asked, slipping between them. "Is everything okay with your neck?"

Doc nodded. "Everything looks good on my end, but I'd like you to evaluate his flexibility at C-five and six again. I'm not sure these numbers are right."

"Definitely." She pointed to the table, her eyes meeting Blane's for a fleeting moment. "Have a seat. I'll be over in just a second. Gabe, I need you to check on—"

Blane shot Dr. Carter a grateful look then sat down and waited for Mandy, plotting his next move.

He wasn't going to let this chance slip through his fingers.

Not with Mandy on the line.

Especially not when he had the feeling that she was it for him.

SEVENTEEN

Mandy

MANDY FINISHED CHATTING with Gabe and was then pulled into the pool room to take a look at another player's knee, and then the conditioning coach wanted her advice on a stretching routine.

She kept trying to get back to Blane but was being pulled in a million directions at once.

And he kept waving her off when she popped over to apologize.

"Go," he said. "Finish what you need to. I'll wait."

But she didn't want to wait.

She'd spent the last twenty-four hours stuck in her own head, replaying their night together, going through the memories of their interactions from the last few years.

Searching for a red flag, for an excuse to not jump.

She hadn't found one.

Yes, he was an NHL player like her dad had been, but that was the *only* thing they had in common. Blane was kind and thoughtful, well-liked by his teammates. He wasn't an alcoholic misogynist like her father had been.

Brit—female, shattering barriers left and right—was his best friend, for fuck's sake.

So she either needed to cut this off at its head or to just jump in and go for it.

And since this was the first time in her life Mandy had struggled to keep up her walls with a man, she was taking it as a sign that things with Blane were different, that *he* was different.

By the time the Gold had hit the ice that evening, she'd mentally shored up her spine and decided she was going to do this.

Fingers crossed it didn't blow up in her face.

After a few more words, she sent the strength and conditioning coach on his way and started for Blane, only to be stopped two steps later by Coach Bernard.

Her eyes met Blane's and he shrugged as if to say, *"What can you do?"*

Bernard only kept her for a couple of minutes, but as much as she wanted to break away from the conversation and go jump Blane, she was also thrilled by what she was hearing.

The board had voted to fund her request for new equipment and another trainer.

They were supportive of her plans—to prevent injuries before they even happened—and were backing her.

The pieces of her life were finally falling into place.

And it was because she'd pushed aside her fear and leaped into something new.

There was a lesson there.

But she was too busy making eyes with Blane to focus on it fully.

"Hey," she said, finally at his side.

A brush of his fingers along her cheek. "Hey, sweetheart."

The spot tingled, and she just stared at him for a long moment before clearing her throat and moving to check the flexibility and muscles on his neck.

"Turn to the left. Now the right," she said after he complied. "Okay, reach your ear to each shoulder." Hmm. There wasn't a digression. In fact, the sides had balanced out even more. "Any pain?" she asked, fingers on his spine as she palpated.

Blane's palm came up to cover her hand. "No." He tugged her forward. "Are you okay?"

Her lips flattened. "*I'm* fine. Why did Gabe—?"

One brow lifted.

Oh.

She'd been had.

Mandy crossed her arms and glared at him.

Blane put his hands up in surrender. "Not my idea. Doc was just throwing me a bone since you've been avoiding me."

"What?" Mandy began cleaning up the stations, throwing away the trash and organizing the supplies back into their proper positions. "I haven't been avoiding you."

There that brow went again.

"Stop." She reached up and nudged it back down. "I'm not lying."

He began ticking off fingers. "Okay, but one, I texted you and you didn't reply. We had breakfast and nothing. Two, you weren't here when I came in this morning. Three, you didn't examine me after the game. Four—"

"Because I was worried if I touched you, I wouldn't be able to stop."

Blane's fingers curled into a fist. "What?"

Her lips curved into a rueful smile. "I want you. I want *us*. I was just worried that if I said something with the room full that I might do something stupid and jump your bones."

"Oh."

"Yeah," she said. "*Oh.* Also, I wasn't here this morning because I was giving a presentation to the board and asking for new equipment, which they approved, by the way—"

"That's great." His eyes lit up before going a little mischievous. "Maybe another hot tub?"

She rolled her eyes. "Considering you all refer to the current one as Ball Soup, I don't think we'll be investing in that."

He chuckled and grabbed her hand. "Seriously, though, that's great." A squeeze. "I'm proud of you."

Tears filled her eyes. For absolutely no reason.

Except maybe, that no one had ever said those words to her.

"It's for new equipment and another trainer," she said, dropping his hand and her gaze to the drawer and straightening the already straightened supplies.

Fingers came to her jaw, tilted her face back up. "That's good news. So why are you crying?"

She shook her head. "I'm not crying." Except, she kind of was. She'd lost her battle with the blasted moisture and teardrops were leaking out of the corners of her eyes.

"Did I do something—"

"*No.*" She sniffed. "Fuck. This hasn't been about—this isn't about *you.*"

He dropped his hand, straightened. "I'm—"

Shit. Mandy grabbed it back, holding his palm between both of hers. "I didn't mean it like that."

Here it came. Here came the secret. The shit that had her so knotted up and closed down inside. Here was the shame, even though she logically knew that none of it was her fault.

"It's not—I didn't mean to hurt you. I just . . . I'm really good at keeping my distance from people." Her laugh sounded broken, even to her own ears. "I've never had many friends. Hell, I only tolerated Gabe in medical school because he took really good notes."

And he hadn't left her alone.

"Then I came here and met Brit, and I felt like we were kind of kindred spirits. We hit it off."

"Not a lot of women around here."

Mandy nodded. "Yeah, but also, she's just really fucking cool. And then I realized you two were friends and that you were in love with her"—he opened his mouth, but she dropped his hand and placed her finger over his lips—"It's okay. I understand now. Hell, I'm half in love with her myself. She's Brit."

He kissed her finger then tugged it free. "Yeah. And I do love her, but after she met Stefan, I finally understood that it never would have worked between us."

She smiled. "They are pretty perfect."

"Sickeningly perfect."

They laughed.

"But you being Brit's friend was a good thing. It made you seem 'safe' and somehow you slipped in under my defenses."

"Well, that," he teased, playing with the end of her ponytail, "and the fact that I'm the sexiest man you've ever seen."

"Just call you Chris Evans?" she teased back.

"*Ouch.*" He slapped a hand across his heart. "I'm wounded."

A snort. "Not hardly. But six months ago, things shifted for me."

"Probably because that's the time I started having wet dreams about you."

"Blane!"

He tugged her down next to him on the table. "You're beautiful, sweetheart. You breathe and I'm hard. I want to bend you over—"

She stood up again, gaze flicking to his lap and then back up. "You've done it now."

"I don't need to do anything," he murmured. *"That's* all you."

Her breath caught. *"Oh."*

Eyes darkening, he stood. "You know how I feel about that sound."

"I didn't mean to."

"Mmm." He rose to his feet, slipped a hand behind her neck—

The door slammed open. "Post-game workout in five," the conditioning coach, Joe, shouted, before letting it crash back closed.

"Fuck," Blane muttered, lowering his forehead to hers. "Sorry."

"We both need to finish up," she said. "It's the job."

"Will you come to my house when you're done?"

She nodded.

He kissed the top of her head. "Thank you." Halfway to the door, he stopped. "So to be clear, you haven't been avoiding me?"

Mandy rolled her eyes. "No."

"And you want to be my girlfriend?"

Her heart skipped a beat, but she brazened on. "Will you give me your letterman jacket?"

"Don't have one, but if I did, it would be yours." A smoldering grin that had her catching her breath. "I can get you a jersey with my name on it though."

"Sold." She lifted a hand as he slipped out of the PT suite. "See you later."

"I'm counting down the seconds."

Then he was gone and Mandy found herself with a hockey-player boyfriend.

Life was really weird sometimes.

EIGHTEEN

Blane

BLANE MADE it through the post-game workout and shower in record time then popped back into the PT suite afterward. The space was empty and dark, so he hurried out to where Mandy usually parked her car.

Also empty.

He was about to go back into the arena when his phone buzzed.

Sorry I didn't text you back.

I was scared.

Frowning, he replied.

I don't want to scare you.

The ". . ." signaling she was typing something began almost immediately after he'd sent his text.

Was. I WAS scared. But I'm not anymore.

Tension he hadn't even realized he had leached out of him. That was good, really good.

His phone buzzed again.

Also, look up, Super Star.

Blane looked up . . . and saw she was standing next to his driver's side door.

Wanna carpool?

He grinned, shoved his phone into his pocket, and strode over to her. "Save on that toll lane?"

"You know it."

"Hi," he murmured.

One half of her mouth turned up. "Hi, yourself."

While he really wanted to kiss her senseless, Blane hit the button to unlock the car and helped her around and into the passenger seat. Then, because he couldn't have stopped himself if he'd tried, he reached over and buckled her seat belt, brushing all of the parts he'd gotten so familiar with the night before along the way.

"*Blane.*"

He closed her door and walked around to his own.

"Let me get that for you," she said when he went to clip in his restraint.

She grabbed the buckle from him and—

Snapped it in place.

But it was her other hand that was the cause of his trouble.

"I can't find it," she teased, fingers running up his thigh.

He snorted. "It's not *that* small."

She cupped him, squeezing tight. "It's not *small* at all."

"Mandy," he breathed. "You're killing me."

"Mmm." She squeezed him one more time then sat back into her own seat. "I hope you have condoms at your house."

THE DRIVE back to his place took an eternity.

Mandy sitting next to him, slanting heated glances in his direction, smelling so fucking incredible, just existing in the same realm as him, and the twenty-five minutes seemed like twenty-five hours.

Finally, he pulled into his garage and shut the door behind them.

Then he shoved his seat all the way back, unbuckled his seat belt and hers, and tugged her onto his lap.

"Bl—"

He kissed her.

Blane slid one hand in her hair and the other down her back to cup his most favorite ass of all time, pulling her hips so she was pressed tightly against him.

She tore her mouth from his on a moan. "Mmm. *Baby*," she panted. "I . . ."

He kissed her again, encouraged her to move against his cock.

Fuck that felt incredible.

Her hands dropped to his seat, gripping the headrest as she rode him. He slipped his fingers under her shirt and up, slipping beneath her bra to her breasts.

"Fuck," she hissed when he pinched one nipple between his thumb and forefinger. "I—that feels—I need—"

He twisted, shoving the material out of the way as he sucked her neglected nipple into his mouth. Her hips bucked, thrusting against him hard enough to make him moan, and he shifted forward wanting—

The horn blared, making them both jump.

Her hazy eyes flashed to his. "What—?"

"Shh," he said. "I got you."

He popped the door open and stepped out with her in his arms.

"Wait—" she began.

"My neck is fine," he said, nipping at her jaw.

"No." She hissed when he sucked hard on the spot. "I need my purse. It has the condoms—"

Blane set her on the hood of the car. "I have one," he said. "Don't worry. I would never *not* use one until we—" He shook his head, cheeks creasing into a smile. "I've got this, okay? Let me take care of you . . . at least for a little while."

She froze, head dropping forward as she sucked in a huge breath. "You don't know what you're asking."

A finger under her chin, deep chocolate eyes locked on hers. "I *know*, sweetheart."

She swallowed hard. "Okay."

"Okay?"

When she nodded again, he kissed her gently, pouring every bit of tenderness he was feeling for this woman into the press of his lips, the stroke of his tongue, the way he held her carefully against him. He scooped her up from the hood, knowing that she needed more than a quick fuck against his car, that she needed him steady and present, that she needed slow and stable and *permanent*.

They'd just revisit the car later.

Because the image of her naked and restless on top of it, him on his knees, between her thighs . . . yeah, that was something he needed to tick off his mental checklist.

Carefully, he made his way to his room and set Mandy on the bed.

His heart skipped a beat, seeing her there, on the mattress, in his home, in his life. He hadn't really recognized how much he'd wanted this, wanted *her*, until this moment.

Last night had been hot, don't get him wrong.

But that moment had felt as though it had an expiration date.

This? *This* felt like the beginning.

He'd played in the finals, had pushed through moments of pressure, had stepped up to sink home a clutch goal in the final seconds of a game. He worked hard and pushed and pushed and *pushed*.

But never with women.

Oh, he'd had his share, especially when he'd been young and on the road and lonely and bored.

Those had been easy, quick expenditures for mutual satisfaction.

Last night had been more than that, but it hadn't been this. The need to make it perfect so that she would see, so that she would stay—

His stomach knotted hard enough for him to lose his breath.

This was important because he loved her.

The feeling had been growing over months, fueling the desperation to batter down her defenses and make her see . . . him.

And now she was there.

She was in his bed, and he had to hope to fuck that he didn't screw this up.

Mandy deserved—

"Hey, Super Star?" she asked quietly, her expression concerned. "Why is there smoke coming out of your ears?"

He froze, realized he'd been staring at her for a good minute. "I'm so—"

"Don't apologize," she said. "Just tell me what's going on."

"This isn't—it's not *easy*."

She grabbed his hand, reclining back on the bed and tugging him along on top of her. "I know."

"It's not simple."

Her palm came up to press above his heart, which was pounding like the beat to one of the rap songs that Max was obsessed with. "I know."

"I'm afraid I'm going to screw it up."

Mandy's hand twitched, fingers digging into his chest before smoothing out. "Why do you think I ran for so long?"

He snorted. "Not *that* long."

"I've wanted you in my bed for an eternity, Blane. I was just too scared to go for it."

"So why now?"

"You know all of those things you just mentioned? All of that . . . this isn't simple or easy, the worrying about fucking it all up stuff?" He nodded. "I realized that I could either stand by and be scared for the rest of my life—pretending to let people in but not actually allowing them to know the real me, not permitting anyone to see who I am deep inside, to give them the chance to judge me and find me lacking. Or—"

"Or?" he asked when she didn't go on.

Her expression softened alongside her voice. "*Or* I could take a chance on the only man who's ever made me want to take off my armor and show him *every single part* of me."

His throat went tight. "Fuck, sweetheart."

She bit her lip. "I know." A pause. "So puck's on your stick, Super Star. What are you going to do about it?"

NINETEEN

Mandy

To SAY that Blane simply kissed her would have been the understatement of the century. He consumed her, filled her veins with fire, with desire, until she threatened to burn from the inside out.

Okay, she was being dramatic.

But with just the press of his mouth against hers, his body, his chest, his *cock* hard where she was soft, she was more turned on than she'd ever been.

He slipped his hand under her head, not breaking the kiss as he rolled onto his back and took her with him. One second she was flat against the mattress and the next, she was straddling his hips, his erection cradled between her thighs.

"Not bad, Hart," she said when they finally broke for air.

She rested her palms on his chest, squeezed two perfect handles of pecs. Yeah, that feeling right there was probably why guys liked boobs so much.

He smirked, and she realized she'd spoken aloud. "It *is* better when you're topless," he said.

"Mmm, *that* I can get behind." Especially considering what Blane did to her breasts when she was half naked. She straightened, tugging off her T-shirt before reaching for the buttons of Blane's dress shirt.

"Me, too." His eyes hadn't lifted above her neck, and Mandy was glad she'd worn her best bra. Lacy and see-through, it pushed her modest set of breasts up and together, giving her a rare moment of legit cleavage.

"You like?" she asked, leaning down to press a kiss to his chest.

"I"—one hand rose to rest on her back and he unhooked her bra—"do like." Both palms cupped her. "But I like this better."

Her eyes rolled into the back of her head. She liked *that* better, too.

But she wanted him naked. And inside her.

But naked first.

Her fingers shook as she undid the rest of the buttons. He played with her breasts, squeezing them gently, teasing her nipples as he did so, distracting her, making her hands slip more than once.

"You're making this hard," she panted, head spinning, thighs clenching, pussy aching.

He flexed his hips, making her moan. "Isn't that the point?"

She kissed him, hard. "Blane?" she asked when she pulled away.

He did something with his thumb and forefinger that had her seeing stars. "Yes?"

"Normally, I'd be all about foreplay and taking our time, but can we just"—her words broke off on a gasp as he thrust up with his hips again—"forget that?"

His fingers slipped beneath the waistband of her pants. "Forget what?"

"Can you, please, just forget foreplay and fuck me until I can't walk?"

He froze, mouth slightly agape. Then he smiled, a slow, scorching grin that had moisture pooling between her legs.

Until he spoke.

Because confusion treaded along the edges of her desire.

"No."

"What?"

He flipped her, kneeling between her thighs and then, in a movement so fast she could barely track it, her pants were off and her underwear pushed to the side.

Blane dove at her, his mouth meeting wet, hot flesh and he gave her a kiss so sensual that she was ramping up the edge to an orgasm in seconds. He spread her wide, laving his tongue over her clit, pressing one finger of his free hand inside of her.

It was too much and not enough.

Too intense. Too little. So much sensation that she threatened to burst through her skin.

And not Blane. Not inside. Not—

He slid in a second finger.

She came with a scream, chest heaving, covered in sweat, her muscles limp as cooked noodles.

"Holy—" Mandy jumped when he flexed his hand, fingers still inside her and making her nerve endings flare to life.

"See?" he asked, pressing a kiss to her clit that had her shuddering. "Isn't that better than me just sticking it in?"

He nipped at her side, soothing the small hurt with his tongue, before slowly making his way up her body as he licked and kissed and bit every inch of her exposed skin.

"Yes," she gasped, gripping his shoulders as he feasted on

her breasts. "But *now* would be a good time to *stick it in*. I want you inside me, Blane."

"Hmm," he murmured against her skin, ignoring her as he kept teasing her.

Which was pretty much the point she'd had enough.

She reached down and grabbed his cock.

"Christ, Mandy." His head dropped to her chest as he pushed into her hand.

"You. Inside. Me." She punctuated each word with a squeeze.

"But—"

Stubborn men. Seriously.

She pushed him onto his back and slid down the mattress, sucking him into her mouth, both hands encircling his erection, taking him deep enough to make him unleash a blistering set of curses.

And she'd pretty much thought her ears were unblisterable.

One stroke. Two—

Next thing she knew, she was back on the pillows, breath whooshing out of her, and Blane was reaching into his nightstand for a condom.

A crinkle as he tore the wrapper open. A moment to roll it on and then he stopped and stared at her.

Her nape prickled, her insides roiled with a combination of desire and fear. She'd succeeded in finally snapping the leash of his control.

He was normally so calm, so together.

But the man staring down at her was neither of those. His eyes were molten, his jaw clenched tight. Every muscle in his body was taut with need. "Last chance, sweetheart," he gritted out. "Last chance for slow and sweet."

Any slice of fear faded. This was her Blane, her hot, sexy,

unhinged Blane. But he was still there, still hers. She gripped his shoulders, yanked him down.

"Enough slow and sweet," she said, clamping her teeth onto his earlobe. "I need hard and fast."

That was it.

A heartbeat later he was inside of her and, *fuck,* did it feel good.

"Better hang on tight, baby," he said and thrust deep.

Her head spun, but Mandy did as he said, and she certainly didn't regret it. Blane stroked in and out in a rhythm that had her nails digging into his shoulders, her moans bordering on screams. He hurtled her to the edge of another orgasm and then . . . arched her back, lifted her hips to meet his.

And exploded.

Or at least, that was what it felt like. Pleasure flowed through her body, and her mind went fuzzy. She was vaguely aware of crying out, of Blane thrusting once, *twice* more before he shouted her name.

It was a long time before she came back to Earth to find him cradling her against him, his fingers stroking through her hair.

She smiled. "See?" she said, her voice slightly raspy after her verbal accolades of Blane's skills. "Even after hard and fast, you still bring the sweet."

His chest shook with laughter.

Mandy stayed pressed against it and lifted her hand, palm up.

Right on cue, Blane high-fived it.

"Go team," she deadpanned.

He chuckled, lacing his fingers with hers. "Go team."

TWENTY

Blane

BLANE WAS MISSING the third movie and trying not to feel salty about it.

So what if it was his favorite of the series? This was more important.

This being waiting in a fragile-looking armchair in the sitting room of Pierre Barie's office and hoping the owner of the team and current acting GM would be able to see him that evening.

He'd begged off on Mandy's party, knowing that it was more of a girl's night than anything and figuring meeting with Pierre was more important.

Life and all its baggage was hard.

The fewer hurdles their relationship needed to clear, the better.

He'd already spoken to Bernard, and obviously Dr. Carter had given his all clear, but he didn't want any barriers between them.

He wanted Mandy to feel safe in breaking things off with him if necessary.

Not that he planned on letting her go . . . but he also didn't want to do anything to risk the career she'd worked so hard for.

More than that, he didn't want her trapped. He wanted her to . . . *choose* him.

So instead of being *with* the woman who'd managed to infiltrate every part of his brain, he was at the arena, dodging fans from a pop concert and waiting for Pierre.

His phone buzzed.

Stefan.

We're coming up now.

Convenient that Pierre was his captain's father and Stefan had called in a favor from his dad for tickets to the concert for their backup goalie, Spence, and his daughter. It put the very busy Pierre in the arena at the right time.

At this point, Blane would take any advantage he could get.

He shoved his phone back into his pocket and stood, trying not to pace as he waited for Pierre to show up.

The handle turned and the door pushed open. Stefan and Pierre strode into the room.

Show time.

"Blane," Pierre said. "Good to see you're up and feeling better. That was quite a hit you took."

They shook hands.

"Doc and Mandy fixed me right up," he said, following when Pierre indicated his office. "We're lucky to have them on staff."

Stefan hesitated on the threshold, but Blane waved him forward. Anything he was going to tell Pierre, his captain needed to hear as well.

"Hiring Dr. Carter and Amanda is probably the single useful thing the previous owner did," Pierre said, sitting behind his desk. "But you're not here to discuss our staffing."

Blane straightened his shoulders. "Actually, we are."

Pierre frowned. "Is there an issue? I haven't heard from your agent—"

"No," Stefan interrupted. "Hang on, Dad. This isn't like that. Blane's here because he wanted to talk to you about something important, and he wanted to do it in person, not through a proxy."

"Oh yeah?" Pierre's face went blank. "Is there an issue with our sports medicine staff?"

"No. I mean *yes*. It's not—" *Shit.* He was fucking this up. "I —" Finally, he just blurted out the truth. "I'm in love with Mandy Shallows."

Stefan raised his eyebrows. Pierre's expression didn't change.

Blane prattled on. "We've both been avoiding each other for months, trying to ignore it, but I can't any longer. She means too much. She's—" He sighed. "She's everything. I can't imagine seeing her every day and not being able to be with her. This isn't a quick fuck because she's here and convenient. Mandy's special. She talented, whip-smart. She has us all in the best shape of our career."

"And if that's true, why would I risk that for a relationship that might implode any second?" Pierre's brows drew together, his blue eyes swimming with irritation.

"I wouldn't if I were in your shoes." Blane swallowed hard, knowing that this meeting wasn't going as he'd planned, but knowing he had to keep trying anyway. "But I also know that while this is my job and I love it and I feel so lucky to be playing for this team, hockey isn't more important than her. If you had to choose between her or me, I'd want you to choose her. Every single time."

Silence.

Pierre stood and turned to gaze out the window. The bright lights of the city shone through in a mishmash of glittering spots.

Shit.

Because there was no response. Just silence.

Blane opened his mouth, about to continue speaking but Stefan kicked his chair. When he glanced back over his shoulder, Stefan shook his head.

Getting the message, Blane sat silently in the chair and waited.

For several long minutes.

Or an eternity.

That too.

Finally, Pierre sat back down in his chair and folded his fingers together on his desk. "That was the right answer, son."

Blane relaxed. "Yeah?"

Pierre nodded. "I appreciate you coming to me, that speaks both a lot about your character and also how important Amanda is to you." He paused, glancing at Stefan before returning his gaze to Blane. "I'll speak to her, but so long as this is her choice, too, I don't have a problem with it."

"And her contract?" he asked. "I believe there's a clause—"

"My guess is that it's time for Amanda to get a raise. And a new contract."

Blane figured that was his cue—to leave, not fist-pump in joy. He stood, extending a hand. "Thank you, Mr. Barie."

Pierre shook it. "I hope your agent will go easy on *your* contract's terms after this."

"Honestly?" Blane asked. "I don't think Prestige Media Group has ever gone easy on any negotiation." He shrugged. "That's why I hired them."

Pierre's lips twitched. "I wouldn't expect anything less from Devon Scott's crew." He winked. "Keep racking up those points, and you won't have anything to worry about.

"Noted."

Pierre's office line rang and he'd barely waved Blane and Stefan off, before snatching it up.

Stefan waited until they'd entered the hall to comment.

"So you love her, huh?"

Blane nodded then waited for the chirp, the joke.

Instead, Stefan just grinned and punched him on the shoulder. "Welcome to the club, brother."

"I'm screwed, aren't I?" Blane asked as they rode the elevator down.

"Totally and royally and in the completely best way possible."

Blane couldn't do anything but smile . . . and pull out his phone to text Mandy that he missed her.

For once, he didn't even tease as Stefan pulled out his, presumably to send the same sentiment to Brit.

The buzz in return, the message in return of *I can't wait to see you later*, was so much better than the buzz from any goal he had ever scored, no matter how clutch.

He was in love with Mandy.

And it felt fucking fantastic.

TWENTY-ONE

Mandy

OKAY, so the sorting hat cupcakes looked a little . . .

"That's disturbing," Brit said, tilting her head.

Mandy tilted her head as well, trying and failing to find an angle the dessert looked appetizing. Maybe it was the globs of black icing or the way it seemed to be slithering off the tops of the cupcakes, but the treats were definitely *disturbing*.

There was something clearly wrong with the frosting.

As in it was melting.

Why was it melting?

She sighed. "I think the icing was too hot when I added the butter."

Sara joined them. "Why was the icing hot?"

Mandy swiped a finger of the frosting up and plunked it into her mouth. Then almost spit it out. Gross. Her buttercream had somehow ended up greasy.

"It's Swiss Meringue buttercream," she said, making a face. "It's supposed to be foolproof. You whip egg whites to stiff peaks and heat sugar up to one hundred sixty degrees. Then you add it—" She broke off when her friends stared at her incredulously. "It seemed easy on YouTube."

"You're insane," Brit said.

"We still love you, though," Sara added.

Brit frowned. "It looks like you tried to murder the Sorting Hat in a vat of acid."

Mandy swiped the platter of cupcakes from the table and dumped them into the trash. "So what if I did?" she muttered.

Monique, sans Mirabel and Spencer who'd gone to a concert at the Gold Mine, gave Mandy a quick squeeze. "Your broomstick pretzels are super cute, though."

"Unfortunately they taste horrid," she said. While tying sour strips around pretzel sticks had definitely given them a broomstick feel, actually eating the combination was a lesson in . . .

Barf.

"They can't be that bad," Monique said, plunking one into her mouth before wincing then chewing with the determination of someone who wasn't willing to spit out a bite of food, no matter how bad.

"Here." She grabbed the trash can and held it up to Monique's mouth, who daintily disposed of the offending appetizer.

"Okay, so they're not good." She plunked her hands on her hips, gorgeous chocolate curls bobbing with the motion. "Where does that leave us?"

Brit held up her phone. "Movies and DoorDash."

Mandy knew when to admit defeat. She trashed the pretzels and put on the first movie as Brit ordered a boatload of Indian food.

The doorbell rang, and Sara opened it, letting in PR-Rebecca alongside Nutritionist-Rebecca. Greetings were exchanged, wine glasses distributed and filled, and then they'd gorged themselves on PR-Rebecca's brownies as they'd waited for the delivery guy.

"I know I'm supposed to be encouraging you to fuel your body with super greens and low-fat protein," Nutritionist-Rebecca said, taking a giant bite of brownie. "But these might be the best things I've ever tasted."

PR-Rebecca waved a hand. "You've spent too long eating that crap to know mediocre food when you eat it.

"You're insane," Sara said. "I'd swear you put drugs in these brownies."

They all froze when PR-Rebecca didn't immediately deny the fact.

"What?" she asked as they stared at her.

"Are these pot brownies?" Brit demanded.

"What?" PR-Rebecca said. "No. Literally, I got the recipe from the Food Network. No leaves in sight—super green or otherwise."

"I," Monique said, "for one, don't care what you put in them so long as you keep bringing them."

"Agreed," Mandy chimed in and got up to answer the door when the buzzer rang. She returned, her arms laden with bags of food, to five pairs of eyes studying her closely.

PR-Rebecca raised a brow. "Do you have something to tell me?"

"What? No."

Except that she was apparently dating Blane.

That he wanted to be boyfriend-girlfriend.

Good grief, that sounded so juvenile.

Surprisingly, it was Nutritionist-Rebecca who outed her. "She's hiding something. Look at her face."

Again five pairs of eyes locked onto hers.

Brit squealed and they all winced. "Holy shit, you did it, didn't you?"

"Did what?" Sara and Monique asked in unison.

PR-Rebecca narrowed her eyes.

"You finally got it on with Blane."

"Wh—" She shook her head. "I—Why is that any of your business?" Ten brows raised in her direction. "Okay, fine. Blane and I are . . . dating."

Brit fist pumped.

"Holy shit," Sara said. "Really? That's great."

Monique grinned and even Nutritionist-Rebecca smiled. And she was normally so serious that it was hard to get a read on her. Maybe PR-Rebecca really *had* spiked those brownies.

PR-Rebecca was the only one without a happy expression. She crossed her arms, tapping her foot on the new floors Mandy had installed. "When were you going to tell me?"

Mandy winced. "Uhhh."

The other woman's brightly painted red lips pulled down. "So that's never."

"I—uh. It's new?" Mandy tried to spin it.

"Hmph." PR-Rebecca pulled out her phone and made a few notes. "With your dad who he was, this might be a bigger story than you expect."

"I won't talk to the media," she said. "Not now. Not ever."

"You might—"

"*No.*"

PR-Rebecca froze, studying her for a long moment before nodding. "Okay. It blows up, I'll take care of it."

"Thank you." Mandy straightened her shoulders and began passing out food. "So am I crazy? It's—I really like him, guys." She bit her lip. "What if he decides—"

"You're not crazy," Brit said. "He's a good guy. You can trust him."

Monique nodded. "And plus, hockey guys are the best."

"I can second that," Sara said.

PR-Rebecca grinned. "He hurts you . . . no brownies."

"I'll gut him if he hurts you." Eyes wide, they all slanted their gazes to Nutritionist-Rebecca, who'd spoken a line that normally would have been straight out of PR-Rebecca's playbook. She shrugged. "What? I just think we all make a good team."

Mandy smiled, heart threatening to burst, thinking she was so lucky to have these strong, capable, funny women in her life.

"*You guys.*" She sniffed.

Brit grabbed the remote, turned up the volume. "No crying until *Goblet of Fire.* That's an order."

The girls seconded that sentiment, and they all began digging into their meals as Mandy sank down onto the couch. She cuddled close to her friends, her container of chicken marsala in her lap.

"Thanks for the push," she whispered to Brit when she took a momentary break from hoovering the delicious food into her mouth.

Brit shrugged, but her lips were curved into a grin. "You're his Ginny."

Mandy grinned back. "Why do I think he would like that comparison?"

"Because we are all big ol' nerds."

"I can live with that."

Brit bumped her shoulder. "Me too."

———

Mandy glanced down at the contract Pierre Barie's assistant had set in front of her in disbelief.

"But that's *double* what my current—"

Pierre steepled his fingers beneath his chin, waiting as his assistant strode out of the office, shutting the door behind him. "Rule number one in negotiations: don't act shocked when someone wants to pay you money." His lips quirked. "Ask for more."

"But—"

"Both Bernard and Dr. Carter sing your praises. Hell, three-quarters of the team have been up in my office swearing by your treatments and begging me to not let you go."

Mandy frowned. She'd been petrified when she'd arrived at the arena Monday morning and Gabe had said Pierre wanted to talk to her.

He'd found out about Blane.

She was going to be let go. She should have known better. Blane couldn't protect her from this. Stefan was allowed to date Brit only because he was the owner's son.

So basically, she wound herself up into a full-blown tizzy by the time the elevator had dinged open on the top floor.

But now she was in Pierre's office and the conversation wasn't going as planned.

"I still have two years left on my current contract."

Pierre switched tack. "Do you want to be in a relationship with Blane Hart?"

Her breath froze in her lungs.

He leaned back in his chair. "Because if you don't, and you're feeling pressured or—"

"No!" she hurried to say. "It's not like that. I swear, neither of us meant for it to happen. It's—"

What? Different? Not a quick fling? Wouldn't affect her job?

All of those.

But also more.

"He's . . ." Mandy sighed, tried to find a way to encapsulate just what Blane meant to her.

Aside from her friends, she didn't really have anyone.

Her mother was wrapped up in her own life, and while Mandy called on holidays and her birthday, the same courtesy wasn't received in return. Her father was gone. She didn't have any siblings. She had Gabe, of course, and Brit, and the girls—

Okay, she wasn't alone. Not anymore. She'd been steadily building her own family since working for the Gold.

But Blane was different.

Even with Gabe, for all the years she'd know and trusted him, she still kept him at a distance.

Yet Blane managed to penetrate all the layers of steel she held tightly around herself.

And he made it look effortless.

Or maybe, he didn't *have* to barge through.

Maybe he made her want to loosen her grip on those sheets of armor.

"He's . . ." She began again before laying it all on the table. "Blane is more important to me than any other person in my life."

Silence.

Now she'd done it.

She'd just screwed them both—

"Check page eight."

"What?"

Pierre leaned across the desk and flipped through the papers before arriving at the eighth page. He placed his finger on a paragraph about halfway down. "Read."

". . . romantic relationships are discouraged between players and staff," she said aloud, her heart racing, "but can be sanctioned by management should extenuating circumstances apply." Her eyes flew to Pierre's. "I—"

"Blane spoke to me," he said, almost gently. Which was a word she'd never heard associated with the notoriously hard-ass businessman before. "But that will mean absolutely nothing if this isn't what you want, too."

Her eyes prickled with tears, and Mandy swallowed hard. "It's what I want," she said with a sniff. "So, so much."

"Good." Pierre picked up a pen and signed his copy then reached across and signed hers as well, leaving the pen in front of her so she could repeat the process. "That's done, then," he said, almost brusquely now. "I'll pass this copy along to the lawyers. Keep yours for your records."

Mandy stood and nodded, knowing that was her cue to disappear. "Thank you, Mr. Barie. I won't forget it."

His eyes dropped to his phone, as though willing it to ring so he could end the conversation.

It didn't, so she hurried out of his office and out into the hall.

That had been excruciating . . . and amazing.

And so she didn't know whether she wanted to kiss or kill Blane.

———

Kiss, she decided once she'd entered her office. Definitely kiss.

A beautiful bouquet of flowers sat on her desk, alongside a note.

Practice this morning at RoboTech.
You staying at my place or am I staying at yours?
-B

The few minutes of terror had been worth it, though she really wished he'd warned her that he was going to talk to Pierre. Yes, it was a logical step if they were going to make a go of their relationship, but a little preparation would have been nice.

It had been like being called to the principal's office.

Not cool.

But considering the end result, she couldn't complain too much.

She and Blane could see where their relationship went without any pressure.

And the money wasn't too bad either.

Smiling, she leaned in to smell a pale pink rose and nearly jumped out of her skin when Max shouted from her doorway.

"Flowers? *Oooo*, who from?"

What had she been thinking about no pressure?

She and Blane were in for no little amount of teasing once they all found out. Which was probably going to be in two point two seconds, since Max had managed to snatch up the note from her desk.

"Your place or mine?" he asked, eyes dancing. "Signed just *B*? Oooo, who could that be? Brit?" He smirked, waggling his brows. "No? Fine. Only in my fantasies, I guess."

She fake-vomited and made a grab for the note. Not that it mattered, since he'd already read it.

"Brian?" he asked. "No. I don't think I've seen a Brian around."

Mandy finally managed to snag the letter and shoved it into her back pocket. "Not Brian." She crossed her arms. "You should go or you'll be late for practice. It's at RoboTech"—the company had sponsored the building of a multi-sheet ice rink for both the team and city to use, and it was where most Gold practices were now held—"No one is here today."

"Except the person who brought you flowers," he said. "Not Brit. Not Brian. Not Bob or Billy. It can't be Blue, he's too young. *Oh*"—his gaze locked onto hers, smile almost blinding —"I got it. Byron."

"Oh my God," Mandy muttered. "That was a poet, not a date. I'm with Blane, okay? It's new and good, and you'll just keep your mouth shut about it until we're ready. Got it?"

Okay, so maybe the finger wagging in his face was a little much, she thought as Max paled and took a step back.

"You're scary sometimes, Mandy," he said, trying to slip out the door.

She stopped him. "Just remember who helps make your workout," she warned.

Max raised his hands in surrender. "I don't know who the B is," he said. "Not a clue until you tell us."

Mandy narrowed her eyes. "That's right. Now hurry up before you're late."

He turned, hesitating before rotating back to face her. "For the record, Blane"—she cleared her throat meaningfully and he jumped—"whoever this *B*-person is. Well, he's a good guy, okay? Don't hurt him."

She had to stop herself from making her *Aw*-face and only just managed to hang on to her serious expression because she knew if she gave Max an inch, he'd take a mile. She'd find both herself and Blane teased mercilessly.

So no. No softening up was allowed.

"Go," she ordered.

He went. Stopped again a few feet away.

"Just so we're clear. I'm still allowed to give Blane a hard time, right?"

Mandy lifted her phone so it was in his view and began typing out a text. "Just so we're clear, you want extra reps of abs today?"

Max hot-footed it to the door. "No teasing. Got it."

"Bye, Max."

"Bye, Mandy," he called adding right before the door closed. "He's lucky to have you, by the way."

It slammed shut, nearly rattling the pictures from the walls.

She shook her head.

But she was smiling.

TWENTY-TWO

Blane

ROAD TRIPS WERE a typical and lonely part of a professional athlete's life.

Players were away from their families, isolated in hotel rooms with too much free time on their hands.

Oftentimes this equated to trouble.

But this time, he was traveling with the person he was in love with.

In love with.

He still couldn't believe it.

He was head over heels, completely gone for Mandy.

A smile spread over his face as she boarded the team's private plane, her backpack slung over one shoulder. She wore a long-sleeved T-shirt emblazoned with the Gold logo, and her ever-present ponytail was tucked through the back of a team hat. There wasn't a lick of makeup on her face, and she wore loose-fitting sweats.

She was beautiful.

And she was his.

As she walked down the aisle, she paused to talk with Gabe then continued back toward where Blane sat. Usually this was the unofficial players' zone, but fuck if Blane was going to sit by anyone but her.

Eighty-two regular season games already meant that free time together was hard to come by.

So he was going to steal every single free second he could.

Mandy paused by his row, eyeing the empty seat next to him, and apparently felt the same way because she asked, "Is that seat taken?"

Since bantering with her was pretty much his favorite thing, he pretended to consider that. "I don't know," he said, tapping his finger to his chin. "I really like to spread out on these flights."

"Hmm," she said, a smirk teasing at the corners of her mouth. "I guess that just means I have to go sit with Blue."

Blane snagged her wrist and tugged her down into his lap. "You're not going anywhere." Her lips were right there, so he kissed her. "Now, do you want the window or aisle?"

She went very still, her gaze flicking around the cabin. He followed her stare, saw that the whole team was watching them, no little amount of curiosity on their faces.

"Did you expect me to hide it?" he asked softly, brushing his knuckles along her jaw.

"No," she said. "I mean, I was coming to sit by you. I just"— she shook her head, a tinge of pink on her cheeks—"didn't expect you to declare it so loudly is all."

He tipped up the brim of her hat so he could see her eyes more clearly. "That bother you?" It was a serious question, but one that he didn't know how he'd be able to address if his actions *did* bug her.

Blane didn't want to have to consider every action with her.

He wanted to be able to hug or kiss or touch the woman he was in love with and not be scared she might not like—

Mandy slung her arms around his neck. "If it bothered me, would I be doing this?" She leaned close to rub her nose along his. "Or this?" She kissed him, long and slow and deep.

Catcalls filled the plane after she pulled back.

"Your affection doesn't bother me, Super Star," she said gently. "But I'm not used to it. If I freeze up—and I probably will—just smack me around."

Never.

"How about I kiss you instead?"

Her laugh made him feel about ten feet tall. "Cheese ball. But kissing, I can agree to." She shoved his shoulder. "Now scoot over. I want the aisle."

The boys teased him as he gathered his stuff and shifted to the other seat, but Blane didn't give a damn.

He had Mandy.

And he was going to keep her.

BLANE TOWELED OFF and slipped back into his suit, wanting nothing more than to be in a pair of sweats and a T-shirt, vegging out with a very not-meal-plan-approved post-game beer.

The game that evening had been a tough one. Their flight had been diverted to another airport because of weather the previous evening, and then their flight had been delayed that morning.

Routine was important to hockey players, and theirs had been all kinds of fucked up.

The delays meant their guys had struggled to get vehicles to transport their gear, and then a traffic jam just outside the city had delayed the buses further. They'd made it by game time, but it had been a close thing, and there certainly hadn't been time for their normal pregame procedures.

It had shown on the ice.

Oh boy, had it shown.

But the game was over now. Tomorrow was another day and all that shit.

Sighing, he shoved his shoes on his feet, grabbed his bag, and left the locker room.

Get him to the bus and the hotel already.

He weaved his way through the arena's hallways, up the stairs, then pushed out the doors and strode over to the bus.

Brit and Stefan were already seated in the back, cuddled up together, and Blane sighed as he sank into a seat in the row next to them.

Lucky bastards, getting to be together all the time.

Brit's eyes flashed to his, her brows drawing together. She whispered something to Stefan then got up and made her way to him.

"Uhhh," she said. "What the fuck are you doing?"

"Tonight sucked," he muttered. "Can we just get back to the hotel and rehash it all tomorrow?"

"We," she said. "Is the key word."

He shoved a hand through his hair, still wet from the shower. "I'm tired and not following, Brit. Just lay it on me."

She huffed, crossed her arms. "Are you or are you not dating Mandy?"

Blane straightened, stomach clenching. "Oh, fuck."

"Yeah." Brit rolled her eyes. "Most boyfriends don't forget their girlfriends."

"I didn't—" He cut himself off because obviously he *had* forgotten Mandy. "Stefan has it easy. You're already here."

"Get your ass off the bus and go grab your girl before you fuck this all up." Brit stepped closer as a few of the guys slipped into their seats. "And I'm only telling you this because you're my best friend, and when you're not being a pouty, obtuse jackass, you're a great guy, but"—her voice dropped further—"she's got abandonment issues, Blane. I don't know all of the circumstances, but she's told me enough." She poked his chest. "So don't ruin this by assuming that you've crossed the biggest hurdles between you two now that this has gone public. We girls are really good at holding on to hurts, at burying them deep, and letting them fester. And we're *really* fucking great at thinking we're totally fine only to have something from our past spring up and dynamite our present."

He slung his bag over his shoulder. "I didn't have it easy either, you know." There had been asshole kids and one particularly shitty bully, not to mention the fact that his parents had gone through several rough patches—his dad had even moved out for a time before they had reconciled. There was also the entire decade of unrequited love for the woman in front of him.

She patted his cheek. "You're cute. But seriously," Brit added when he opened his mouth to snap at her, "there's normal. *We*"—she pointed between them—"had normal life shit that was thrown at us." Her eyes darkened. "Or maybe a little more than normal at times, but I think Mandy has us beat, you know?"

Guilt swamped him because, *fuck*, he'd seen the shadows in Mandy's eyes. He *knew* Brit was right.

"Yeah." He clenched his hands into fists. "I don't know the whole story yet, but I think she damn well does have us beat."

"Me, too. So"—Brit pointed to the door—"go. Before you really fuck things up."

Blane squeezed by her, thankful for the kick in the pants, though it hadn't felt good. "Thanks, Bestie," he said and tugged her ponytail.

She batted his hand away then punched his shoulder. "I'm still waiting for my half of the heart necklace."

"You're getting better with your chirps," he retorted as she moved to sit beside Stefan again.

"Never let it be said that I don't work on all aspects of my game."

He snorted and hurried off the bus.

Pierre was talking to Coach Bernard. They broke off their conversation as he strode by.

"I'd hurry if I were you, son," Pierre said.

Bernard nodded. "In Dr. Carter's office, last I saw."

Blane started running.

TWENTY-THREE

Mandy

MANDY TOOK the iPad out of Gabe's hands. "I'll finish the reports. Go," she urged when he started protesting. "Your mom is waiting." With his job on the West Coast but his family on the East, Gabe didn't get to see them much, and she knew he worried about his mom, who was recently widowed.

"I don't like leav—"

"*I'm fine*," she said. "Just exhausted after today's craziness." Hours on the plane, followed by hours more on a bus.

But she'd been by Blane's side, so it had been more of an adventure than a trial.

Until now.

Gabe bent to meet her eyes. "You sure that's all it is?"

"Yes."

He crossed his arms. "And it's not the fact that Blane isn't here?"

Yes. *Yes*, of course it damn well was. He'd all but declared himself to the team and then . . . forgot her. "He's busy with the team," she said, hating that he'd made her feel like this.

Like her dad used to.

"I'm good," she said, shoving that feeling deep down and pushing Gabe out the door. "Seriously. I'll just finish with these and then head back to meet Blane."

Nice words, but would that actually happen?

Of course, it would. This was just a weird day with extenuating circumstances. With all the delays and the subsequent rushing around, they hadn't had a chance to talk about what would happen following the game. Plus, they hadn't been on a road trip together as a couple. There were bound to be quirks to work out.

A total misunderstanding.

That was it.

But she couldn't put out of her head that—plans or not—he'd always come before.

Maybe Bernard had pulled him into a last minute meeting?

She bit her lip and started scrolling through the reports on the iPad, archiving some as old, healed injuries, marking others as priority cases, reading through and updating treatments that had been completed that evening.

A knock on the doorframe and Pierre popped his head in. "Sorry to interrupt, but have you seen Dr. Carter?"

Mandy stood. "I sent him on"—she glanced at her watch—"maybe twenty minutes ago now? He had family in the building."

"Okay." A beat. "Will you pass along that I'm heading out of the country for two weeks? Terry will be here in my place." Terrance Freidman was a former player, present assistant GM, and currently being groomed to take over GM duties from Pierre—who while a good owner and GM, had more business than sports experience.

Then there was the complication of him being Stefan's dad.

"Will do," she said. "Thank you again for the . . ." She shook her head. "I just really appreciate the funding for my requests and the new contract. And Blane," she added. "Thank you for understanding."

He nodded. "It's good business. Nothing more. Happy, healthy players, happy staff. That part isn't rocket science."

"Pierre—"

"Sorry," Bernard said when he came equal with the doorway and realized he'd interrupted. "I didn't mean to intrude, but did you need a few minutes? The bus is loaded and the players are ready to go."

Mandy's stomach clenched. "Was—?"

"Blane?" Bernard glanced over, eyes softening. "Last I saw, he was leaving the locker room. I'm sure he'll be over—"

"Of course," she said and held up the iPad. "But don't let me keep you from your meeting. Pierre, I'll be sure to pass on your message to Dr. Carter. Thank you again. For everything."

Pierre's brows drew down, but he nodded and both men said their goodbyes before walking down the hall and disappearing out of sight. Her eyes flicked to the locker room door, currently wide open as the equipment staff hurried in and out.

They had to walk by the office she was in to exit the hall.

Just as the players had needed to.

Just as Blane had to.

So why wasn't he there yet?

Sighing, she sank down into the chair and forced herself to focus. He would come or he wouldn't. God knew she'd spent too much of her childhood waiting for her father to show up.

He rarely had.

The single good thing she'd learned from those experiences was that she *couldn't* sit and wait. She had to do *her*. Had to live her life and not put everything on hold.

Like her mother had. Like *she* had for ages.

Well, not anymore.

Mandy was going to finish these reports, catch a car to the hotel, and then spend an hour in the tub with a book. She might even splurge on room service.

Yes. A twenty-dollar sandwich would make everything just perfect.

She sniffed.

"Dammit." Huffing, she wiped the tears away and tried to keep her focus on the reports. This was her job, a job that she'd just been given a raise for and in that moment, she was bawling like a baby, not even able to finish some fucking reports.

"Ugh." Mandy used her palms to wipe her eyes then inhaled and released it slowly.

It sucked to be forgotten.

She could just leave it at that.

Shove away the hurt and focus on the indignation. She deserved to be remembered, for fuck's sake. She was important. She was valuable.

This wouldn't be like it had been with her dad.

No. She wouldn't let it.

"Okay," she whispered and blew out another breath. "Just— I'll be okay."

The reports came back into focus. She scrolled through them, making adjustments and notes, doing her job like a fucking adult, thank her very much.

She'd just saved the reports to the team's cloud and stashed the iPad into her backpack when her phone buzzed. It took a minute for her to dig it out of the bottom of her bag, but when she saw the lock screen showed a text from Brit, her heart both leapt and dropped.

Because if she was being truthful, Brit was *not* the person she wanted to hear from.

And then the screen flashed with an incoming call from her mother.

Fuck. Her. Life.

"Okay, drama queen," she muttered to herself. "Man up and answer the phone." She gave herself one more second before swiping a finger across the screen. "Hi, Mom."

"You're in town and you don't call?"

The gut punch was real.

Those were the words her mother used to say to her father, before he'd gotten hurt, before every single moment of her mother's day had been dedicated to his care, his appointments, the exact fucking brand of socks or carrots or laundry detergent he preferred.

Her father had been a paraplegic and yet he'd still been able to control the women in his life.

Her mother. *Her.*

And this call felt like a fucking blast from the past, the perfect karmic reminder that she was letting a man determine *her* moods, affect *her* day, put *her* through the emotional wringer.

But Blane was different.

Or was he?

"I'm sorry, Mom. I'd hoped to meet up with you, but there was an issue with the plane and—"

"I'm lonely, Amanda."

She dropped her head to the table, felt like banging it repeatedly. "How's tennis going?"

"The women are mean there."

"Oh, did you—"

"And I don't like sweating. It's too hard."

"What about the quilting class I signed you up for?"

Her mother *pfted.* "Did you know that you have to make

sure all of the lines are perfectly straight before you sew? It's impossible."

"Mom, you can draw on eyeliner in a perfectly straight line the first time, every time. That seems like the perfect activity. Plus, no sweating."

"I don't like it."

She imagined her mom sticking out her bottom lip, affecting the little girl persona she'd always taken with her dad.

Because, yes, her dad had been an alcoholic asshole who'd cheated and been his own biggest fan, but her mom wasn't a fucking angel. She was needy, couldn't make a decision before jumping back and forth a dozen times. She liked everything. She liked nothing. She couldn't do a damned thing without a helping hand.

And so every few weeks, Mandy found herself in a conversation such as this.

Except, this time she'd done it to herself

She had thought that if she could only find her mother a hobby, then she would get busy and focus on someone else.

Her mom needed a project and that project needed to be far, far away from Mandy. She'd spent too long trying to be okay without her parents, with never being good enough or smart enough or exacting enough. Just because her father had died didn't mean that she would take his place in micromanaging her mother's life.

And yet, here she was, arranging sewing classes and tennis lessons.

She was seriously screwed up.

No. She didn't want her mother to be unhappy. That made her a good person. But she couldn't also open herself up to be hurt by her all over again. Hell, she'd spent as much time during her childhood chasing her father's approval as her mother's attention.

"How about the makeup classes?"

"You mean doing makeup for those gross old ladies at the home?" her mother asked, obviously affronted.

Fuck it.

Mandy banged her head against the table a couple of times for good measure.

"Mom. I'm tired, and I have a job to do." She sighed. "I'm living my own life, okay? You need to find something to fill yours."

"Baby, I want to—"

"To clarify, *I'm* not the piece to fill yours." Mandy let her head fall back, keeping her eyes shut as she held the phone to her ear. "I can't be your filler for dad, okay? It just hurts too much."

Let her think that it was because she missed the old bastard, rather than the fact that she wasn't willing to open that part of her heart up again.

Too much had happened.

"Well, I—" her mother sputtered.

Mandy had learned, growing up in a dysfunctional, co-dependent, booze-filled, angry, and resentful household meant that she had to embrace every means to protect herself.

Which meant cutting ties at some point.

For her own health and sanity, she needed to keep her mother at a distance.

"Goodbye, Mom."

She hung up then read the text from Brit.

He's an idiot. But not an idiot on purpose.

Mandy snorted, ready to write a reply when she felt it.

Or rather, *him.*

TWENTY-FOUR

Blane

HER EYES WERE sad and rimmed with red.

Fuck.

"Sweetheart, I—" He took a step toward her, gut clenching when she put a palm up to stop him.

"Hold on." Her shoulders rose and dropped on a sigh. "I need to say this."

He stopped, nodded. "Okay."

"You hurt me tonight. A lot," she said then lifted her chin and straightened her shoulders. "But I don't think it's exactly fair for me to be mad and hurt and miserable about it without you knowing why it affected me so much."

Blane reached out a hand. "Can you at least let me hold you while you tell me? I can't stand that look on your face, can't stand knowing I hurt you, unintentionally or not, without trying to at least make you feel better."

Mandy froze.

Then her shoulders crumpled and she began sobbing.

Those tears were like acid to his soul. He strode forward and took her into his arms, knowing she hadn't okayed it but not able to let her cry alone.

"I'm sorry," he murmured over and over again.

She buried her nose in his chest. "It's not you exactly. I—I just—" She sniffed and took a deep breath. "I talked to my mother and then with you not being here, all of the shit from my past is super fresh. I was scared to date you because you're a hockey player and my dad was one, and he was a total asshole." Her words rushed together, and Blane struggled to follow. "He drank so much, but that part wasn't even the worst. It's like he got off on these mindfuck games."

Her hair was in her face, so he brushed it back, cupped one cheek. "Like what?"

"Like he'd promise to come home and then wouldn't"— brown eyes locked on his—"but it wasn't that he forgot to come home or something. He'd get a kick out of making us wait and wait and *wait*. Sometimes he'd call and say he was coming, for my mom to change into a certain outfit, and then he'd turn around and head out to a bar."

He couldn't help the frown that pulled his brows together, but he hesitated to ask—

"I know that sounds like I'm just mad because he got caught up with the team or the rink or something, but I would literally watch his car pull in to the driveway. He'd wait until my mom rushed to open the door, and then he'd just stare at her a moment before driving away."

"Fuck," Blane muttered.

The Roger Shallows he and the rest of the world knew was a charismatic and gifted player. He'd color commented many a game after his career-ending injury, had always come off as upbeat and fun to be around.

Hell, there hadn't even been a rumor of being difficult floating around locker rooms.

Everyone loved the guy.

"I know," Mandy said. "And then later it would be because she wasn't wearing the exact outfit he asked for or that he left because I didn't get straight A's or eat my food right or—"

She broke off. "It was never enough. No matter how good my mom and I were, it was never enough."

He tilted her face up. "And after?"

Her expression tightened. "Worse than before. He wasn't playing but would disappear for days at a time, blow off doctor's appointments he demanded my mom set up. And he drank"—her laugh was brittle—"fuck, I'm surprised he wasn't a pickle for as much as he drank."

"Shit, Mandy," he said. "I had no idea."

She swallowed. "No one does. I mean, the only good thing really is that he never brought us around the team, so a lot of people don't know that I'm his daughter, and I don't have to pretend much."

Her fingers traced a button on his shirt as he asked, "Is your mom better now that he's—?"

"Gone?" she asked. "No. Of course not, because she was as bad as he was in a lot of ways. She'd be furious with me when he left, yell at me, hit me, and tell me it was my fault, that I wasn't perfect enough, pretty enough, whatever." A shake of her head. "I tried for a long time to live up to those expectations, but who could? No matter what I did, there was *always* something I was doing wrong."

He touched her cheek. "I understand now why you didn't want to date me."

"Well," she said, her words quiet. "*That*, and it was a convenient excuse in a lot of ways. You're pretty scary."

"No," he said fiercely, understanding fully now what Brit had been trying to tell him on the bus.

Mandy was maybe the toughest woman he knew, and he knew a lot of strong women—his mother and best friend included. But Mandy had not just endured and carried on and succeeded in a world that was typically male-dominated. That alone would have garnered his respect.

Knowing her past just made that admiration for her grow so much more than he thought possible.

She was the woman he loved, but also an incredible woman in her own right.

"No," he said again when she opened her mouth. "I mean, I get the scary, yes. I know it's frightening to put yourself out there." He brought her hand to his heart. "But *this* beats for you. I know I'm just a normal guy who had two parents who loved each other, who was picked on at school occasionally, who may have had his heart stomped on a few times. I know I've been so, so lucky, sweetheart. I haven't had to endure what—" His throat tightened and fuck, his eyes stung. "I'm so sorry you had to go through that. But I also feel so incredibly lucky to have you in my life."

"Blane . . ."

"And I hate that—"

She kissed him gently. "Thank you. For being angry, for caring that I was hurt." Her eyes went serious. "But I need you to understand that what happened tonight can *never* happen again. I can't be someone's afterthought, can't wait around wondering if you might turn up. It might be completely unreasonable, but I just can't be in a relationship with someone who doesn't consider me a priority." Her lips pressed flat. "Logically, I understand that it has nothing to do with mind games with you, but I'm messed up, Blane, and tonight my mind started going to this really dark place, and I just—"

"I get it," he said. "And it's not unreasonable or unfair. Forgetting about you was unforgivable, even without knowing what happened to you."

Her gaze dropped to where her palm still rested on his chest. "I'm sorry."

He gripped her face in his palms. "Tell me again why in the fuck you're apologizing? You were upset, shared why it hurt you so badly, and are asking for what you need. Isn't that called adult communication?"

She bit her lip. "I don't like it. I don't *want* to be an adult. I want to binge on *Harry Potter* and sleep in way too late."

Blane chuckled at her petulant tone. "Next day off and we are so doing that."

She laughed and he relaxed, tugging her close so he could hug her tightly.

Eventually, she pulled back. "Thank you for understanding." A pause, her lips curving as she held up her phone and showed him Brit's text message. "You're also apparently an idiot, though not one on purpose."

He snorted. "There's my best friend, always standing up for me." With that, he helped Mandy to her feet. "Should we go back to the hotel?"

"Only if you're sharing your bed," she said.

"As if that was in question." He touched a fingertip to her nose, wanting to tell her how he felt, almost desperate with the need to declare his love for her. But this wasn't the right time, and he didn't want what they were building to be tainted by the past. "Anything of mine is already yours, sweetheart."

She stared at him for a moment, her expression soft, then turned to grab her bag, glaring when he took it from her and slung it over his shoulder.

But instead of protesting, she just sighed, laced her fingers through his, and squeezed.

Three times.

"I need a bath," she said.

He leered at her, waggled his brows. "Seeing you naked? Now *that* can be arranged."

Her giggle made him feel ten feet tall.

TWENTY-FIVE

Mandy

"Okay, I lied," Mandy said, rolling over in her bed and handing Blane the remote. "I want to binge watch that flat earth documentary on Netflix. Brit said it's insane."

Blane, one arm behind his head, shirtless, and yummy chest on display, took the remote with a smile. "Blasphemy! You promised me magic and really evil wizards. What the hell?"

She climbed on top of his chest, heart full, happier than she'd ever been.

These last two weeks with Blane had been incredible. Also, insane with the extended road trip followed by two games at home. Then there had been a dinner for the Gold Institute—the charity the team supported that funded local sports and education, and *then* that night was Sara's gallery opening.

But for now, she was enjoying a PJ Sunday with Blane and bad TV.

His hands dropped onto her hips, the controller pressing into her side.

She snagged it back from him and flopped onto the mattress. "Fine." Mandy gave her best impression of evil villain laughter. "I take back control of the television then."

He tickled her side in response then drifted his fingers lower, making her alternatively squeal then groan in pleasure. "How about we watch the documentary later and instead"—a brush of his thumb between her thighs—"we make some magical sparks in the here and now?"

Mandy froze and stared at him, one brow raised.

"It wasn't that bad," he protested.

"It was bad," she replied, smirking at him. "Really, *really* bad. Cheese ball bad, so awkward it was totally cringe-worthy bad."

"I—" His objection cut off when she grabbed his free hand— meaning the one that was not currently between her thighs— and brought it to her breast.

"And while it might have been absolutely terrible," she said. "I'm still willing to make some *sparks*."

He snorted then grumbled, "Who's the cheese ball now?"

Her hand snaked down to his erection, which was doing an admirable job of bursting free of his boxer briefs.

"I want you inside me." A squeeze to punctuate her statement. "Is that better?"

Blane rolled on top of her, dropping his mouth to hers, kissing her so intensely that Mandy felt as though her heart would beat out of her chest. Her skin went tight, her thighs clenched, and her nipples tingled, aching for him.

God, but could the man kiss, she thought as they broke away for air.

Every time, every *single* time he pressed his mouth to hers, she was transported, taken away to a place where it was just the two of them in the universe, where the rest of the world couldn't intrude. Every kiss was special and different and meant something.

There was only one explanation for the way he made her feel.

She loved the man.

Only, how to tell him? How to take that leap when all of her love had always been tied up with the fucked-up shit from her past?

What if she could *never* say it?

A finger tapped the middle of her forehead lightly. "What's going on in that big juicy brain of yours?"

She winced. "That I'm screwed up?"

His brows drew down and he rolled to his side. "Sweetheart."

"No"—she grabbed at his shoulders to tug him back over her —"come back. It's not like that and *plus*, you asked what thoughts were in my mind. They're not always going to be, *Blane's so amazing!*"

His expression turned affronted.

"No," she hurried to say. "Ah geez. I *do* think you're amazing. I was—That is—dammit, Blane, I was thinking that I loved you so much and that I had no clue how I was ever going to tell you because I'm so messed up, and—"

He stilled, half on top of her.

Mandy realized what she'd said. "I know it's too soon, and I—"

His lips pressed to hers, giving her one of those kisses that made her forget all of the bad thoughts swirling through her head and focus on the way he made her feel—cherished, precious . . . loved.

He was smiling when he pulled back. "Had to outdo me, huh?" Blane tucked a strand of hair behind her ear. "I've been trying to find a way to tell you that I love you for weeks. But I thought it was too soon and didn't want to scare you off."

She wrinkled her nose. "I think, based on the facts, you should be scared off by me."

His eyes rolled heavenward. "Should we just both admit that we're scary?"

Taking a moment to consider that, she nodded. "Yes. Yes, we should."

"Okay. We're scary," he said. "Also, I love you."

Yikes. But also, holy shit did that feel incredible. He loved her. Blane Hart loved Mandy Shallows.

And she hadn't been struck down by lightning or anything.

A smile split her face. "Also, I love you, too."

"There you go again," he teased. "Outdoing me in the declaration department."

Her brows drew together in a frown. "Because I said I love you, *too*?"

"No," he said. "Because when you say those words, you make me feel like the most important man in the world. You make me feel like I could climb Mt. Fucking Everest, just because you asked. You make all of those holes in my heart, the missing pieces, the jagged edges disappear." He brought her hand to rest above his heart. "You make me feel *more*. With just those three words, I become somebody."

"You're somebody, Blane," she said, feeling his heart pounding beneath her palm. "You've always been somebody."

"Maybe." His fingers tangled with hers. "But you've made me somebody who's finally living instead of waiting on the sidelines, watching everyone else find their slice of happiness."

"Yes," she whispered. "I understand."

Because that was exactly what Blane did for her in return.

TWENTY-SIX

Blane

BLANE WAS WEARING A SUIT, and it wasn't even a game day.

He smiled over at Mandy, who was dressed in a gorgeous dress Monique had brought over that afternoon.

Having been kicked out of the apartment, Stefan, Mike, Spence, and Blane had found themselves at loose ends. They'd ended up getting a beer and watching some basketball on TV at a local bar while the girls had taken over Mandy's apartment for their own personal version of *Say Yes to the Dress*.

Yes, he was now intimately familiar with the show.

No, that didn't make him pussy-whipped.

Or maybe it did, and he just didn't give a damn.

Either way, he was propped against a wall, a beer in one hand, his eyes locked on his woman, when he felt a tap on his shoulder.

He turned, expecting a fan and was shocked to see his mother.

"Mom?" he said stupidly. He hurried to hug her. "*Hi*. I didn't know you were coming into town."

"Brit invited me." Eyes similar to his own narrowed. "*She* invites me to things."

Blane shook his head. "Nice try with the guilt, Mom. But I believe I extended an open invitation even before the season started, and you told me work was crazy."

His mom worked for the FBI in a very classified and highly demanding position.

Her lips twitched. "Maybe."

"I'm glad you're here," he said, dropping an arm over her shoulders. "And I like your dress."

She patted her hips. "This old thing?" But she smiled anyway.

It was odd now, thinking about how hard his mom had worked when he'd been a kid—hell, she *still* worked insane hours—but he'd never felt resentful of the time she'd been away. She had always tried to come to everything important, to be home for dinner, for games, and school plays, even if she had to return to work afterward.

Why had Mandy's dad not done the same?

Was it because *his* dad, whose job was significantly less demanding, had been accepting of the time his mom had spent at work while Mandy's mom had made it a huge battle with Mandy forced to play a pawn?

They both had similar stories in a way—one parent gone a lot with a demanding career, while the other picked up the slack at home.

Why had his childhood been great when *she'd* been dealt a shitty hand?

"I can hear the wheels turning, baby," his mom said, startling him out of his thoughts. "Everything okay?"

"I'm fine. Just thinking about when I was a kid."

"Is it because of Mandy?" she asked.

His eyes flew to hers. "How do you always know?"

"I work for a very powerful government organization."

He fixed her with a look. "You mean Brit told you."

A shrug. "Sources are an important part of intelligence."

"Unbelievable."

Brit glanced over then and gave an awkward wave. He sent her a glare in return. "Yes, it's because of Mandy. I love her."

His mom tucked her arm in his. "Come outside for a minute. I want to talk to you."

They walked through the exhibit and out onto a patio. The air had a bite to it. When his mom shivered, Blane slipped out of his coat and placed it on her shoulders. God, but the city was beautiful sometimes, or maybe that was seeing it through the lens of Sara's artwork. She had a way of capturing the buildings and lights and traffic and transforming it into something beautiful.

"Sara's very talented," his mom said.

"Yes." He nudged her arm. "But that's not why you dragged me out here and stole my coat."

"You're a good boy, Blane," she said. "Always have been, and I'm proud of you."

Uh-oh.

"Why does that sound like the other shoe is about to drop?"

"Well"—she winced—"kind of because it is."

"And this is about Mandy?"

His mom nodded. "I ran her."

"You background checked my *girlfriend?* What the fuck, Mom?"

She put her hands up. "I background check all of the girls you date . . ."

Which had been pathetically few, but still. "Mom!"

"You never know what some of those women might want. You're a wealthy man, an athlete. I'm trying to protect you."

"Protect me?" He scoffed. "And you're telling me that Brit put you up to this?"

"No. I mean—*yes*. Yes, she told me you were dating someone and that I should come out and meet Mandy because she was great and things looked serious, but I did the background check all on my own. That wasn't Brit's idea." She lifted her chin, touching his arm. "You're *my* baby, Blane. I—"

"Invaded my privacy," he said, furious. "You did this behind my back."

"Well—"

"That's *not* okay, Mom. I love you. *Shit*." He pulled away. "But you don't get to do that."

He hadn't really ever been mad at his parents. Sure, there was the usual teenage strife, pissy about not being able to go to a party or being allowed to spend time alone with a girl. But he'd been too busy and focused on hockey to care all that much.

Especially since they'd let him play hockey as much as he had ever wanted.

So not much room for conflict there.

But *this* was different.

His mom had delved into Mandy's life, something that was so painful and vulnerable that his forgetting to meet up with her had dredged it all up again and driven her to tears just a few weeks before.

"Look, Mom," he said. "Mandy and I have talked about her past, about *my* past, as boring as that is. I already know everything she's wanted to share." He shook his head. "If there's anything else, then she'll tell me on her own terms and we'll get through it. Together. But you can't do this—you can't cross that boundary and expect that I'll be okay with it."

"Don't you want to know what I found?"

"*No.*" He made a noise of disgust and strode over to the railing, clenching it tightly enough that he was half-surprised it didn't shatter under his grip. "*I don't.*"

"I do."

Mandy's voice made him panic. *Shit.* How much had she heard?

TWENTY-SEVEN

Mandy

SHE HADN'T MEANT to overhear. Really.

But when she'd asked where Blane was and had been told the patio, she hadn't expected to find he'd gone off with another woman.

She'd thought he needed fresh air, a break from the stuffy room.

And she'd wanted to surprise him.

Imagine her surprise at coming up to the door, Blane's arm laced with the gorgeous blonde.

She didn't look old enough to be Blane's mom, but the conversation had quickly transmuted the slice of betrayal she'd been trying to stifle into admiration for her man spending quality time with his mom into shock and horror and . . . so much more admiration.

He'd stood up for her.

Stood by her.

"I do," she said again from the doorway. "I'd like to know

what you found out that was so important it warranted a trip across the country."

Part of her was furious. How dare his mom do that? Part of her was hurt. Would her parents' screwed-up relationship never just stay in the past? And part of her was curious. Growing up, nothing had ever been transparent—it was all mind games and hidden meanings and—

Well, she'd rather know all of it. Now.

Both of them had frozen when she'd spoken, Blane turning in almost slow motion, a look of horror on his face.

She crossed to him, grabbed his hand, and squeezed. Three times.

Rising on tiptoe, she whispered. "You know that means I love you, right?"

His lips curved. "Outdoing me again?"

A shrug. "It's a gift."

His fingers brushed her wrist. "I'm sorry. I—"

She just squeezed his hand three more times, heart pulsing when he did the same in return.

God, she loved this man.

Then she blew out a breath and turned to face off with his mother.

"Hi, Mrs. Hart," she said. "I'm Mandy, though I guess you already know that."

Blane's mom extended a hand for Mandy to shake. "Allison." Her tone was, rightfully so, chagrined. "It's lovely to finally meet you."

"Yes," Mandy agreed. "Though maybe we can skip the formalities just this once, and you can tell me what it was that brought you out here."

Allison sighed. "Okay. But I do want you both to know that I really did come because I wanted to meet you. I had a conference in the city that lined up with Blane's schedule, so I wanted to watch him play and meet the woman that Brit has been raving about."

"But?" Mandy asked.

"But then the background check came in."

She pressed her lips together. "Yeah."

"You know your father—"

"Was an alcoholic abuser? That my mom wasn't—*isn't*—a peach? Yeah. I lived through that touching story the first time."

Allison's eyes softened. "Oh, sweetie. I'm sorry you went through that. I"—she sighed—"it wasn't right for them to treat you like that. You deserved better."

Mandy sniffed. "Don't do that."

"Do what?"

"Be nice and genuine. I'm trying to stay mad at you for invading my privacy."

Allison laughed softly. "I really *am* sorry. I know that I shouldn't have done it, but I am glad I did. And not just because I thought I was protecting Blane, but because I found out something that you really should know."

Mandy glanced up at Blane. He shrugged. "It's up to you."

Her chin dropped to her chest, and she inhaled deeply. Should she ask?

Did she really have a choice *not* to?

Dammit.

Because no.

Blane had told her his mom worked pretty high up in the government. If Allison was here saying what she'd found out was important, then it was.

"Tell me." Mandy straightened and waited for the blow.

"You have a sister."

She blinked, the statement about as far from anything she could have ever imagined. "Uhh, what?"

"Your dad—"

Mandy put her hand up. "Oh, my God. Sorry, just give me a second."

Holy fuck, she'd expected money laundering or something, not *Jerry Springer* type shit.

Blane cupped her cheek. "Are you—?"

She nodded, breathing out carefully. "Okay, freak out semi-averted. How old is she?"

"Twenty-seven."

Gut punched. Hard enough to stall her lungs.

Two years younger than her. Two *fucking* years.

"Sweetheart," Blane said, crouching down in front of her. Somehow, she'd ended up bent at the waist and fervently thanking the fact that the tight dress was made of stretchy material and she hadn't just ripped an ass seam in front of Blane's mom.

Ass seam?

Fuck.

She began laughing. This was completely unbelievable and yet not at all surprising.

Of course, her dad had another kid.

Of course.

She blinked hard and straightened. "And did he do the same stuff to her—"

Allison nodded. "I'm afraid so. He was just smart enough to have them both sign NDAs before he passed. No post-mortem scandals."

Mandy pressed her fingers to her temples. "Did my mother know?"

"There is no indication of that one way or the other."

"And is this girl—is my sister okay?"

"Yes," Allison said. "She seems to be doing exceptionally well. She works for RoboTech."

"Here?"

Allison inclined her head. "At the San Francisco office, yes."

"Oh, sweet baby Harry." Allison's brows pulled together. "Sorry, it's a movie reference. I just—" Mandy shrugged helplessly. "I'm just a really big nerd."

Allison's mouth twitched before straightening out. "Are you okay?"

"Oh God, I don't know," she said. "I *think* so. I mean, I guess it doesn't *surprise* me, exactly, because my dad was . . . well, my dad. But I just can't believe I didn't know until now."

"I'm sorry I was the one to have to tell you"—Allison raised both palms—"Look, I *know* I shouldn't have pried. But consider this me making penance for me prying." She reached into her purse and pulled out a piece of paper. "Her email and cell if you want to contact her."

Mandy took the slip.

Angelica Shallows
555-555-1234
ashallows@robotech.com

She had his last name.

Un-fucking-believable.

Allison lifted her arms. "Can I hug you now?"

"Mom. *No*," Blane said.

Mandy snorted but patted his arm reassuringly. "Come here." And she embraced Blane's mother.

Because drama brought people together?

No. Because Allison had cared enough to come here and make sure Mandy knew the truth. That was enough for a hug . . . and maybe more. Maybe they could build something that she'd never had with her own mother? Maybe they could have something truthful and real and—

"Thank you for telling me," she said and pulled back. "But

I'm going to need a promise from you that you won't do any more prying."

Allison made a face but nodded. "I promise." A pause. "But I reserve the right to check up on any boyfriends or girlfriends my future grandchildren may have."

Mandy felt her chin drop.

Blane muttered a curse and said, "Christ, Mom. You're not helping my case any. I want her to stay, not run for the hills."

Mandy smiled and shook her head. Somehow, the thought of little Blanes running around didn't scare her as much as it probably should. She touched Allison's arm. "Future baby background checks are up for discussion at a later point."

Allison grinned and clapped her hands together. "Grandbabies!"

"Now you've done it," Blane grumbled to her, before adding, "She said later, Mom. As in at a *much later* point."

Allison ignored him and grabbed Mandy's arm. "Let's get back to the show before we miss anything exciting. And then I think I owe you and Blane dinner for all the trouble I caused."

Mandy turned, glancing back over her shoulder at the man she loved.

"For the record, I didn't say *much* later," she said, half because it was the truth and half because she wanted to see his response to the words.

His jaw dropped, but then he grinned and hurried to catch up to them. Allison shrugged off Blane's coat as they entered the exhibit, shoving it at him so she could rush over to Brit, no doubt to share the gossip.

Blane took the jacket but didn't put it on. "Not much later?" he asked, brow raised.

"How about semi later?"

He brushed a thumb over her cheek. "That sounds perfect."

TWENTY-EIGHT

Blane

"ARE YOU OKAY?" Blane asked a few hours later.

Their bellies were full of good food and drink, their minds full of Sara's amazing art, but he was worried about Mandy.

His mother.

Fuck.

First, he couldn't believe that she'd run a background check on the woman he loved and second, he couldn't believe what she'd found out.

Mandy had a sister. One who was only two years younger than her.

Her father was even more of an asshole than she'd known.

And yet Mandy was lying next to him in bed with a smile on her face.

"I'm fine," she said, snuggling closer. "I mean, I think I'm okay. Like I said, it's . . . not surprising, I guess."

Considering her dad had been an absentee, cheating father, that was true.

"I just"—she began tracing circles on his chest—"do you think she might want to know me at all?"

Blane slid down until they were face to face. "She'd be a fool not to."

One half of her mouth turned up. "You're too sweet."

He scoffed. "I'm exactly the right amount of sweet, thank you very much." A brush of his thumb across her lips. "But I think if you want to contact your sister, then you should. Worst case, she's not interested in getting to know you. Best case, she is and is someone you want in in your life."

Mandy nodded. "You're right, of course, but I don't think I'm ready yet."

"Your terms, sweetheart," he said. "You get to decide if and when you're ready to reach out. And that can also be never. We've got a good group of people around us. Hell, my mom wants to take you shopping before she goes home."

A snort. "Only because Brit refuses."

"Maybe." He chucked her chin. "But also because she knows you're a good person."

"Ugh." Mandy sniffed. "Why do you do this to me?"

He slid his hand to her ass. "Grope you?"

"Be so fucking perfect. You're everything I ever hoped for." She sucked in a breath, dashed a tear away, then shot him a mock-glare. "But all these emotions you make me feel. Also," she said, shooting him a grin after he'd wiped her tears away with his free hand. "Let it be noted that I like the groping."

He squeezed, tugging her closer to his side. "I'm good with groping."

"Also, I love you," she said. "Even despite your mom being kind of cuckoo for Cocoa Puffs."

"I'm still so furious that she did that. I swear, if she ever crosses that line again I—"

Her lips found his. "No," she ordered when they broke

apart. "She did it because she loves and worries about you. I'm *glad* you have someone who cares about you that way."

He rolled his eyes. "Just wait until you meet my dad."

"I'm looking forward to it." Her hand snaked down. "But let's discuss your parents later."

Blane's eyes rolled into the back of his head. "Yes." He groaned when she slid down and her mouth teamed up with her hand. "Later."

THE SEASON FLEW BY, and before they knew it three months had passed.

And that only meant one thing: playoff time.

AKA, he was living and breathing hockey.

Of course, Mandy had been breathing it alongside him, pulling longer days with the team as the brutality of the eighty-two-game season took its toll and injuries became prevalent. The team was in fairly good shape overall, but even the healthiest player couldn't go out on the ice night after night for months on end without experiencing at least a minimal amount of bruises and strained muscles.

Blane was no exception, having taken a puck high up on his chest just the night before.

But he had his personal physical therapist.

"You're all black and blue," she said and *tsked*. "Did you even put ice on this?"

Blane raised a brow.

"Okay, fine," she muttered, smoothing some cream on his skin before buttoning up his shirt. "Of course, you put ice on it. But, babe, you're lucky you didn't break a collarbone."

"That's what Doc said." Blane rolled his shoulders and bit

back a wince. "But you've trained me well, sweetheart. I'm fine. It's not broken, and I can deal with a bruise."

"*We* can deal with a bruise," she reminded him.

"We," he agreed. "We'd better go before we run late for the bus."

They had stayed at Mandy's apartment the night before since it was closer to the arena—where the bus would pick them up and take them to the airport.

"Yes. Let's hit it," she said, shrugging into a sweatshirt. Blane grinned, making the innocuous statement into a euphemism and she shook her head. "Sicko."

A tug of her ponytail. "You like my sick tendencies." He smirked. "You also like when I *hit* it."

"Oh, my God. You are *such* a dork."

"It's one of my best characteristics."

She laughed and even though it was zero dark thirty—okay, so it was only sixty-thirty in the morning—his heart still felt so fucking full.

Mandy did that. She just filled him with so much love and joy—

"I love you," she murmured.

"My line," he said and leaned down to kiss her.

Her eyes filled with tears before she shook her head and closed the door behind them. "Don't make me cry, Blane. You know I get emotional during playoff season."

He snorted. "And they say I'm the dork."

"I say. *I* say that." She locked the apartment and started down the hall. "I am a little emotional, I guess, though," she said as they hit the stairs. "I've been feeling all out of sorts."

Blane froze mid-step. "Holy shit, are you pregnant?"

"What?" Her jaw dropped open. "*No.* I mean, I don't think so. We haven't—I'm on birth control."

If he was honest, her not being pregnant gave him the slightest pang of disappointment. "Oh, okay."

She frowned, glancing at her stomach as they continued their way down the stairs.

"What is it?" he finally asked.

"Have I put on weight or something?" She tugged at the hem of her sweatshirt.

Shit. "No, baby." He scrambled, trying to unfuck his words. Impossible, considering what he'd said. "It's just that you said you were feeling off and emotional and—"

They pushed through the door into the garage. "And what?" she asked.

"And"—he winced—"we have a lot of sex."

Mandy stopped. Then smacked him on the chest.

Right on the bruise.

He hissed and she frowned, probably because she hadn't hit him that hard.

"Oh shit," she said, tugging at the collar of his shirt. "I didn't mean—"

It only took him a second to trap her hands and haul her close. "Sweetheart, I'm fine. Big, tough hockey player, remember?"

She snorted but didn't fight his hold.

"And you're as beautiful as ever. We've been together for a bit now, and . . . I guess I wouldn't be opposed to it."

"What you're saying is that it's semi-later?"

He brushed back her hair. "Yes. *That.*"

"And that your parents want grandbabies?"

"God, yes." He groaned, thinking of the sheer amount of times his mother had inferred that marriage should be happening soon and babies coming shortly thereafter. Or babies first.

She wasn't picky.

"We should wait until the end of the season."

His heart skipped a beat. Because this was very adult and mature and *fuck*, he so wanted Mandy to have his babies.

"You'll have to marry me first," he said.

She stiffened, and Blane cursed mentally. He'd pushed too hard. *Ha*. What was new?

"Or not," he said. "I just want to be with you, baby. *Only* you."

She slipped out of his arms, started walking for the car. "We need to get moving. And for the record," she added. "I'm not opposed to marrying you, so that better not have been your fucking marriage proposal."

His stomach unclenched.

"It's not." He opened her door, helped her in.

"Good." She smiled up at him. "Because, with you, I want it all."

Blame it on the early hour or the pregnancy misunderstanding, or maybe the almost botched marriage proposal, but they were already driving to catch the bus by the time he remembered to ask her to clarify why she had been feeling out of sorts.

"I emailed my sister." She wrinkled her nose. "I know it's not a big deal and I shouldn't expect an immediate response when I had several months to get used to the idea of her, but . . ."

"You kind of expected an immediate response?"

Mandy shrugged. "Yeah. I shouldn't have, but yeah, I did."

"And," he said, turning into the arena and parking. "So you've discovered you're normal."

"Charmer." She punched him on the shoulder. "But, yes, you're right. I get it. But enough serious stuff," she said and turned to grab her bag from the back seat.

As usual, he beat her to it, throwing it over his shoulder.

"Men," she muttered and got out of the car.

He met her at the front of the hood. "We take care of each other. Get used to it."

Her lips twitched. "I *am* used to it. Doesn't mean I'm going to skip a chance at grumbling this early in the morning, especially when I'm cranky."

"I like you cranky." He took her hand as they walked for the bus.

Once aboard they went their separate ways for the drive to the airport. He sat in the back with the players and Mandy used the short drive to discuss any outstanding issues with Gabe.

The plane was a different story.

Mandy was his good luck charm—he was coming off a regular season with the most points ever—so she would sit by him.

"Blane," she said as he turned to take a seat in the back.

He stopped.

"For the record, I will *so* marry you."

The bus was silent, as was typical this early in the morning, so every single member of the Gold—player and staff alike—heard Mandy's declaration.

As she'd known they would.

Someone whistled, there were catcalls, and no small amount of hoots, but then she kissed him and the world faded away.

At least until Max poked him in the ribs. Hard.

Blane broke away, panting.

"Get a room," Max growled, shoving past them.

Mandy raised her brows, but Blane just shrugged. Max had been surly for the last few months. It would pass.

Mike called, "You buy him a ring yet, Mandy?"

"I heard he likes princess cut diamonds," Blue added.

The chirps continued, and he bopped her on the nose. "So much trouble for that."

She grinned. "For the record, I like princess cut, too."

One more kiss before he strolled to the back of the bus, knowing that so long as he had this woman in his life, he would be okay.

Brit raised her brows.

He waved her away. "Long story. I haven't proposed, but I'm going to."

"Yes!" She fist-pumped then grinned and said, "You better get some pointers from Mike, because he set the proposal bar really high."

Blane punched Stefan on the shoulder. "That what you did?"

His captain only smiled, revealing nothing.

Mike, on the other hand, leaned in and nodded. "That's a yes. The key is to know what's most important to your woman and run with that." He pretended to pat himself on the back. "I know. I am the proposal guru."

Blane rolled his eyes. "Well, proposal guru, here's what I was thinking . . ."

TWENTY-NINE

Mandy

Mandy smelled a rat.

Or rather, a proposal.

But considering it was July and the season had been over for two months—the Gold making it to the Western Conference finals but no further—she'd smelled a proposal at every dinner date and gathering of their friends, so she knew she was being silly.

Still, Blane had called, asking her to meet him at their favorite restaurant—a burger joint on the Peninsula that was super campy in its décor but had, hands down, the best hamburgers in town.

She was almost there when her phone rang.

Frowning when she saw it was Gabe calling, she quickly accepted the call on her Bluetooth. "Gabe?" she asked. "Is everything okay?"

"I need you to come to the arena, there's an issue."

Her heart sank. They were supposed to be completing the

construction of the new PT suite that week. A major issue meant delays, and they couldn't have delays.

"What's wrong?"

His voice sobered. "It's better if you come see."

Shit.

"Okay. I'll be there in ten. I'm actually pretty close," she said and hung up. "This had better not be my proposal being ruined by a leaky pipe or something," she muttered.

Sighing, she dialed Blane's number and quickly explained the situation.

His ready agreement at her putting off their date told her that no proposal was planned that evening. She tried to tell herself that she wasn't disappointed, but that was a lie.

They'd already pulled the goalie—meaning she'd stopped her birth control and they'd ditched the condoms—and so she might already be pregnant.

She didn't really care about being married . . . except it was Blane and she wanted *all* the things with Blane.

A wedding and a white dress. Little hockey players running around their house.

Plus, he'd said—

"It doesn't matter," she reminded herself and turned into the arena parking lot.

The lot was full, but she managed to snag a spot right in front. Rushing, she grabbed her purse and hauled ass down to the PT suite, which—

Was finished?

Her breath caught as she walked in and she blinked back tears. The room was so pretty and full of so many tools.

Gabe stood to one side, his cell in his hand, a smirk on his face.

She crossed to him. "You jerk. I was panicked."

"Don't blame me," he said. "Blame him."

And then he pointed behind him.

Blane strolled out of the newly expanded weight room, along with every current Gold player and some of the former. Even both Rebeccas, Monique, and Sara were there.

"What—?"

They crowded into the room, each holding a rose, huge grins on their faces.

Blane was wearing a suit, a huge bouquet in one hand, a ring box in the other. He walked over to her.

Mandy was crying already. She could feel the tears streaming down her cheeks.

"I'm sorry it took so long, but I wanted to wait until everyone could get back together. I wanted all of your family here with you."

Her family. Yes, these people meant more to her than her own family ever had.

"Oh my God. *Blane.*"

He handed her the flowers and, robotically, she took them, but could hardly spare the bouquet a glance. Her eyes were on Blane.

Who had kneeled before her and opened the box.

It held a huge princess cut diamond ring.

"Mandy," he said. "When I open my eyes in the morning and see you there next to me, I think I'm the luckiest guy in the world. You are so fucking smart and beautiful, and I can't imagine a world that doesn't have you in it." He took her hand, pressed it to his chest. "*This* beats for you. Only you. Will—"

"Yes!" she cried and launched herself into his arms.

Everyone crowded around, cheering and chirping in equal parts.

"You didn't let me finish the question," Blane teased, wiping the tears from her cheeks after he'd slipped the ring on her finger. "What if I had been asking for extra ketchup?"

She squeezed him tight. "No matter the question," she said, "the answer would have always been yes."

The team let them hold each for approximately one more second before they tugged her and Blane apart, and congratulatory hugs and back slaps were shared all around.

Which was just the way it should be.

The Gold was her family.

It was as simple as that.

EPILOGUE

Max

MAX STOOD on the perimeter of the crowd, edging toward the door.

Yes, he was an asshole to escape in this moment, but Blane and Mandy wouldn't miss him.

Plus, he'd been here for the big moment, after all.

No one would even know he'd gone.

He cracked the door and slipped out into the hall.

Then nearly mowed down a tiny little fairy.

Okay, not a fairy, but a woman with pale amber hair and a curvy little body. Some players were about the statuesque model type, but not Max. *He* liked them curvy, and he certainly didn't mind them small.

That meant he could more easily lift them up and they could wrap their legs around his hips while he—

Fuck. It had been a long time since he'd been with a woman.

And this tiny, voluptuous angel was trying to make a quick getaway.

"Hey," he said, snagging her arm when she would have slunk down the hall. "You lost, sweetheart?"

Shoulders straightened and she ripped out of his grip. "Don't touch me," she snapped, keeping her back to him, and *fuck*, even her voice made his cock twitch.

"Okay. No problem." He slid around to her front. "But this area is off limits."

Her gaze stayed on the floor, her jaw clenched tight. "I was invited."

"Oh?" Max crossed his arms, leaned back against the wall. Sexy voice, banging body—he was desperate now to see her eyes, the shape of her nose, her lips. Please let her be as pretty as she sounded. "By who?"

Finally, she looked up.

Max sucked in a breath as though he'd been gut-punched.

Those eyes. They were—

"Mandy Shallows," the woman said. "I'm . . ." She hesitated then lifted her chin and said, "I'm her sister."

Mandy had a sister? Holy shit.

But something was off. Max took a step closer to her, noted that the tip of her nose was slightly rosy, her lids reddened and puffy. "Why don't I think those are happy tears for her engagement?"

The woman pushed around him, striding down the hall before stopping and hanging her head again. "I didn't mean to intrude," she said. "I—" Her voice caught. "She said anytime, but I should have called first. This wasn't mine to witness." A sigh. "If she saw, if she's upset, tell her I'm sorry."

She started walking again, this time faster.

"Wait," he said and caught her arm again. "I'm sure Mandy will be happy—"

"*No.*" She yanked out of his grip, her purse slipping down

her arm and falling to the floor. The contents went every which way.

"Shit," he muttered. "I'm sorry." He knelt to help her, but she batted his hands away.

"Just go, dammit! Just leave me the fuck alone."

"Okay—" he began but didn't get the chance to leave.

Because she'd snatched up her things and was gone.

Sighing, he turned back toward the PT Suite. He should probably face the music. Congratulate the couple, break the news of Mandy's sister running off.

He took a step and the crinkle made him freeze.

Max bent, picked up the paper that must have fallen out of the woman's purse. It was an email addressed to . . . Angelica Shallows.

Fuck, if that wasn't the perfect name for the beautiful *fleeing* angel he'd just met.

—Boarding, Gold Hockey Book #4 is now available.

GOLD HOCKEY SERIES

Blocked

Backhand

Boarding

Benched

Breakaway

Breakout

Checked

GOLD HOCKEY

Did you miss any of the Gold Hockey books?
Find information about the full series here.
Or keep reading for a sneak peek into each of the books below!

Blocked
Gold Hockey Book #1
Get your copy at books2read.com/Blocked

Brit

THE FIRST QUESTION Brit always got when people found out she played ice hockey was *"Do you have all of your teeth?"*

The second was *"Do you, you know, look at the guys in the locker room?"*

The first she could deal with easily—flash a smile of her full set of chompers, no gaps in sight. The second was more problematic. Especially since it was typically accompanied by a smug smile or a coy wink.

Of course she looked. *Everybody* looked once. Everyone

snuck a glance, made a judgment that was quickly filed away and shoved deep down into the recesses of their mind.

And she meant *way* down.

Because, dammit, she was there to play hockey, not assess her teammates' six packs. If she wanted to get her man candy fix, she could just go on social media. There were shirtless guys for days filling her feed.

But that wasn't the answer the media wanted.

Who cared about locker room dynamics? Who gave a damn whether or not she, as a typical heterosexual woman, found her fellow players attractive?

Yet for some inane reason, it *did* matter to people.

Brit wasn't stupid. The press wanted a story. A scandal. They were desperate for her to fall for one of her teammates—or better yet the captain from their rival team—and have an affair that was worthy of a romantic comedy.

She'd just gotten very good at keeping her love life—as nonexistent as it was—to herself, gotten very good at not reacting in any perceptible way to the insinuations.

So when the reporter asked her the same set of questions for the thousandth time in her twenty-six years, she grinned— showing off those teeth—and commented with a sweetly innocent "Could've sworn you were going to ask me about the coed showers." She waited for the room-at-large to laugh then said, "Next question, please."

–Get your copy at books2read.com/Blocked

Backhand
Gold Hockey Book #2
Get your copy at books2read.com/Backhand

Sara

"Sorry I messed up your sketch," he rumbled.

She nibbled on the side of her mouth, biting back a smile. "Sorry I stole your hand for so long."

He shrugged. "My mom's an artist. I get it."

Well, there went her battle with the smile. Her lips twitched and her teeth came out of hiding. If there was one thing that Sara had, it was her smile. It had been her trademark in her competition days.

Which were long over.

Her mouth flattened out, the grin slipping away. Time to go, time to forget, to move on, to rebuild. "Thanks," she said and extended a hand.

Then winced and dropped it when her ribs cried out in protest.

"You okay?" he asked, head tilting, eyes studying her.

"Fine." And out popped her new smile. The fake one. Careful of her aching side, she shrugged into her backpack. "I've got to go." She turned, ponytail flapping through the hair to land on her opposite shoulder.

"That—" He touched her arm. "Wait. I *know* I know you."

She froze. That was the second time he'd said that, and now they were getting into dangerous territory. Recognition meant . . . no. She couldn't.

There had been a time when *everyone* had known her. Her face on Wheaties boxes, her smile promoting toothpaste and credit cards alike.

That wasn't her life any longer.

"Thanks again. Bye." She started to hurry away.

"Wait." A hand dropped on to her shoulder, thwarting her escape, and she hissed in pain.

"Sorry," he said, but he didn't release her. Instead, he shifted his grip from her aching shoulder down to her elbow and when she didn't protest, he exerted gentle pressure until Sara was facing him again. "It's just that know I *know* you."

No. This wasn't happening.

"You're Sara Jetty."

Her body went tense.

Oh God. This was *so* happening.

"It's me." He touched his chest like she didn't know he was talking about himself, and even as she was finally recognizing the color of his eyes, the familiar curve of his lips and line of his jaw, he said the worst thing ever, "Mike Stewart."

Oh *shit*.

—Get your copy at books2read.com/Backhand

Boarding

Gold Hockey Book #3

Get your copy at books2read.com/Boarding

HOCKEY PLAYERS HAD the *best* asses.

No pancake bottoms, these men—and *women*—could fill out a pair of jeans. She wanted to squeeze it, to nibble it, bounce a dime—

Mandy dropped her chin to her chest, losing sight of the Sorting Hat cupcakes she'd been pondering.

Blane with his yummy ass had a unique way of distracting her.

No, it wasn't even distraction, per se. He had *always* been able to get under her skin.

And that was very, very bad for her.

"Ugh," she said, tossing her phone onto her desk and standing, knowing that she wouldn't be able to sit still now.

Nope, she needed about forty laps in the pool and a good hard fu—

Run, her mind blurted, almost yelling at the mental voice of her inner devil. *A good hard run.*

Unfortunately, the cajoling tone wasn't completely drowned out. *Some sexy horizontal time with Blane would be more fun—*

But the rest of the enticing words were lost as the roar of the crowd suddenly penetrated through the layers of concrete. Her stomach twisted. Mandy could tell, even before her eyes made it to the television, that it wasn't in celebration of a goal or a good hit either.

This was fury, a collective of outrage.

She was on her feet the moment she saw the prone form lying so still face down on the ice.

Her gut twisted when she spotted the curving line of a numeral two on the back of the player's jersey.

"Not him," she said and the words were familiar, a sentiment she had whispered, had *prayed* a thousand times before. She needed the camera angle to shift, for her to be able to see more clearly *who* was hurt. "Not him."

Then Dr. Carter was on the ice and the player moved slightly, rolling away from the camera, giving a full shot of his back and the matching twos adorning his jersey.

Fuck. Not him. Not Blane.

And that was when she saw the pool of blood.

—Get your copy at books2read.com/Boarding

Benched
Gold Hockey Book #4

Get your copy at books2read.com/Benched

Max

He started up the car, listening and chiming in at the right places as Brayden talked all things video game.

But his mind was unfortunately stuck on the fact that women were not to be trusted.

He snorted. Brit—the Gold's goalie and the first female in the NHL—and Mandy—the team's head trainer—would smack him around for that sentiment, so he silently amended it to: *most* women were not to be trusted.

There. Better, see?

Somehow, he didn't think they'd see.

He parked in the school's lot, walked Brayden in, and received the appropriate amount of scorn from the secretary for being thirty minutes late to school, then bent to hug Brayden.

"I'll pick you up today," he said.

Brayden smiled and hugged him tightly. Then he whispered something in his ear that hit Max harder than a two-by-four to the temple.

"If you got me a new mom, we wouldn't be late for school."

"Wh-what?" Max stammered.

"Please, Dad? Can you?"

And with that mind fuck of an ask, Brayden gave him one more squeeze and pushed through the door to the playground, calling, "Love you!" over his shoulder.

Then he was gone, and Max was standing in the office of his son's school struggling to comprehend if he had actually just heard what he'd heard.

A new mom?

Fuck his life.

—Get your copy at books2read.com/Benched

Breakaway
Gold Hockey Book #5
Get your copy at books2read.com/BreakawayGold

Blue

"Thanks for the ride."

"Try not to go out and get a fresh bimbo to ride tonight. I hear STIs on are the rise in the city."

Blue sighed, turned back to face her. "Really?"

She shrugged, smirk teasing the edges of her mouth, drawing his focus to the lushness of her lips. "Just watching out for Max's teammate."

He rolled his eyes. "Not hardly."

"Okay, how about I'm trying to prevent you from spreading STIs to the female populace."

"I'm clean, and I'm smart," he told her. "Condoms all the way."

"Ew."

Except there was something about the way she said it that made Blue stiffen and take notice. Because . . . he stared into her eyes, watched as the pale blue darkened to royal, saw her lips part, and her suck in a breath.

Holy shit.

"You're attracted to me."

Her jaw dropped. "No fucking way," she said, too quickly, pink dancing on the edges of her cheekbones. "You're delusional."

Blue got close.

Real close.

Anna licked her lips.

And fuck it all, he kissed that luscious mouth.

—Breakaway, www.books2read.com/BreakawayGold

Breakout
Gold Hockey Book #6
Get your copy at books2read.com/Breakout

PR-Rebecca

A fucking perfect hockey fairy tale.

Shaking her head, because she knew firsthand that fairy tales didn't exist outside of rom-coms and occasionally between alpha sports heroes and their chosen mates, Rebecca slipped through the corridor and stepped onto the Gold's bench.

Lots of dudes in suits—of both the boardroom *and* the hockey variety—were hugging.

On the ice. Near the goals. On the bench.

It was a proverbial hug-fest.

And she was the cynical bitch who couldn't enjoy the fact that the team she was with had just won the biggest hockey prize of them all.

"I knew you'd be like this."

Rebecca turned her focus from Brit, who was skating with the huge silver cup, to the man—no, to the *boy* because no matter how pretty and yummy he was, Kevin was still a decade younger than her—leaning oh so casually against the boards.

"Nice goal," she told him.

A shrug. "Blue made a nice pass."

And dammit, the fact that he wasn't an arrogant son of a bitch made her like him more.

She nodded at the cup. "You should go have your turn."

"I'll get mine," he said with another shrug.

She frowned, honestly confused. "You don't want—"

Suddenly he was in front of her on the bench, towering over her even though she was wearing her four-inch power heels. "You know what I want?"

Rebecca couldn't speak. Her breath had whooshed out of her in the presence of all that sweaty, hockey god-ness. Fuck he was pretty and gorgeous and . . . so fucking masculine that her thighs actually clenched together.

She wanted to climb him like a stripper pole.

"Do you?" he asked again when her words wouldn't come. "Want to know what I want?"

She nodded.

He bent, lips to her ear. "You, babe," he whispered. "I. Want. You."

Then he straightened and jumped back onto the ice, leaving her gaping after him like she had less than two brain cells in her skull.

The worst part?

She wanted him, too.

Had wanted him since the moment she'd laid eyes on the sexy as sin hockey god.

"Trouble," she murmured. "I'm in *so* much fucking trouble."

—Breakout, www.books2read.com/breakout

Checked

Gold Hockey Book #7
Get your copy at books2read.com/Checked

"Rebecca."

She kept walking.

She might work with Gabe, but she sure as heck wasn't on speaking terms with him. He'd dismissed her work, ignored her contribution to the team. He'd made her feel small and unimportant and—

She kept walking.

"*Rebecca.*"

Not happening. Her car was in sight, thank fuck. She beeped the locks, reached for the handle.

He caught her arm.

"Baby—"

"I am *not* your baby, and you don't get to touch me." She ripped herself free, started muttering as she reached for the handle of her car again. "You don't even like me."

He stepped close, real close. Not touching her, not pushing the boundary she'd set, and yet he still got really freaking close. Her breath caught, her chin lifted, her pulse picked up. "That. Is. Where. You're. Wrong."

She froze.

"What?"

His mouth dropped to her ear, still not touching, but near enough that she could feel his hot breath.

"I like you, Rebecca. Too fucking much."

Then he turned and strode away.

—Checked, coming March 29th, 2020, www. books2read.com/Checked

ALSO BY ELISE FABER

Checked (March 29th, 2020)

Chauvinist Stories

Bitch (Feb 16th, 2020)

Cougar (March 1st, 2020)

Whore (March 15th, 2020)

Life Sucks Series (all stand alone)

Train Wreck

Phoenix Series

Phoenix Rising

Dark Phoenix

Phoenix Freed

Phoenix: LexTal Chronicles (rereleasing soon, stand alone, Phoenix world)

From Ashes

KTS Series

Fire and Ice (Hurt Anthology, stand alone)

ABOUT THE AUTHOR

USA Today bestselling author, Elise Faber, loves chocolate, Star Wars, Harry Potter, and hockey (the order depending on the day and how well her team -- the Sharks! -- are playing). She and her husband also play as much hockey as they can squeeze into their schedules, so much so that their typical date night is spent on the ice. Elise is the mom to two exuberant boys and lives in Northern California. Connect with her in her Facebook group, the Fabinators or find more information about her books at www.elisefaber.com.

 facebook.com/elisefaberauthor

 amazon.com/author/elisefaber

 bookbub.com/profile/elise-faber

 instagram.com/elisefaber

 goodreads.com/elisefaber

 pinterest.com/elisefaberwrite

Made in the USA
Monee, IL
09 February 2022

90939634R00121